Chaos & Courtship

The Chronicles of Addison Schmidt – Book Three

Cassidy K. O'Connor

For my mom, Patti, you will beat this, you have the strength of the whole family behind you.

To all the women out there, make sure you get your TaTas checked - it might just save your life.

To my sisters, Jennifer & Sheri, thank you for being there when I need you.

To Terri A. Wilson, I couldn't have done these books without your guidance. Thank you for all your help in making Addison the best witch she could be.

ADDISON STARED at the chaos around her. How could she help someone before the ticking time bomb went off? She ducked out of the way as a stuffed bear flew past her head. Nutmeg was in the battle of his life, and the child screaming behind her would make her, or more likely Minnie, do something everyone would regret.

She closed her eyes and took a deep breath. It was never good when she tried to use magick while her emotions weren't in control.

How had they gotten here?

An hour ago everything had been fine. They'd arrived at the airport and made it through security relatively unscathed. There was an embarrassing moment when the security agent was going through Luna's bag and her vibrator had turned on. Addison had never seen a man turn that shade of red before.

Somehow Nutmeg, spelled to look like a French bulldog, even managed to stay quiet while Luna stammered and rushed to shut *Big Jim* off. Xavier ever the gentleman, grabbed her other stuff so she could get out of there as fast as possible.

Addison dropped to her knees and got Nutmeg's attention. He was at the entrance of the dog carrier with all four paws stretched out as he tried to grab onto the sides so Luna couldn't push him inside. He acted like they were sending him to his death. Once he went in, he was never coming back out. "Listen, I'm sorry, but we booked one of the only airlines that makes dogs ride in carriers for the duration of the flight. I promise when we land, I'll make it up to you."

His adorable little Frenchie face scrunched up. "You are going to owe me big time."

Xavier walked over and sighed. "Sorry big guy. I tried to get them to let you ride in our laps, but they aren't budging."

A panicked squeal from one of the obnoxious kids had Addison spinning around. The little boy behind Minnie was scratching at his face, where his mouth was sealed shut. Minnie leaned back in her chair with a devilish smile on her face.

Addison ran over and undid the magick and the boy's mouth was back to normal right before his mom turned to check on him. His chin quivered for a second before he sobbed and threw himself against her.

Minnie looked way too pleased with herself. Addison glared at her as she dropped into the seat next to her. "You can't do things like that. That boy is probably traumatized for the rest of his life."

The world's worst emotional support witch rolled her eyes. "Good. He was being obnoxious. I swear, if they are near us on the plane, I'll turn them into frogs."

"So we can listen to them ribbit for seven hours?"

Minnie smiled brightly. "Good point. I should pick a quieter creature. How about slugs?"

Addison's jaw dropped. "Seriously, I was kidding."

Luna plopped into the chair on Minnie's other side. "I'm mostly against violence, but even I'm ready to strangle these kids."

Addison looked at the mother of three with her dark under eyes. She was clearly doing her best, but

Addison had three boys close in age. She knew how exhausting that was. An idea came to her, but her magick wasn't reliable enough for her to try anything. "Luna, when we get on the plane, you could do a spell to help them all sleep, couldn't you?"

Luna pursed her lips as she thought about it. "I've not really done a sleeping spell before. I think I could do it, though."

Minnie let out a heavy sigh. "Fine. I can do it. It would be a lot easier and more satisfying if they were slugs."

Addison threw an arm around her shoulders. She saw through the tough witch facade. "Thank you. I would consider it a personal favor."

The speaker overhead crackled as the announcement was made for them to board.

Xavier picked up the carrier with Nutmeg inside it. "Ready ladies? Oh, and if you check your app, you'll see you all have new seats."

What did he do now? Addison opened her boarding pass and saw she was 1A, Luna was 2B, and Minnie was 2A.

Luna held her phone up. "Doesn't the lower number mean better seating?"

Minnie hopped up. "Sure does. We've been

upgraded to first class. There's no way that family will be behind us now."

Addison cleared her throat and waited.

Minnie rolled her eyes. "Yeah, yeah, I'll still knock them out..." Addison cocked her head, waiting, "gently, I'll knock them out gently. Geez, I'm not a monster."

They lined up at the gate. Addison nudged Xavier. "What's with the upgrade?"

"There was no way I was riding for seven hours in coach. Honestly, no one should have to be that cramped for that long."

"Do I want to know how much we owe you?" She was going to have to do a few extra shifts at the coffee shop to pay him back. It had to be a thousand each easily.

"I know I don't scream money, but trust me, I don't need any of you to pay me back."

Well, well, another layer to the mysterious Xavier. Addison couldn't wait to meet his brother and get a better idea of him. Lord knows he didn't share anything.

As the door to the boarding tunnel opened, Luna grabbed Addison's arm, and they squealed quietly. Luna had never been on a plane before and Addison had never ridden in first class. It's sad to admit, but she thought at her age and a divorcee that her chances for adventure were likely over. Thanks to magick, she had a whole new life to look forward to and hopefully she'd find more answers than questions in Scotland. Given how the last few months have gone, she wasn't too optimistic. What surprise was waiting to ambush her?

ADDISON SAT DOWN EXCITEDLY and wiggled her butt in the plush seat cushion. First class really did have it better. What bullshit.

Minnie and Luna got in their seats and Xavier put Nutmeg's carrier in the seat next to Addison before sitting in the chair across the aisle and next to Luna. Addison's jaw dropped. "You bought a seat for Nutmeg?"

He shrugged. "When I bought the upgrades, I didn't know yet that he would have to be in a carrier the whole time. I figured all our lives would be a lot easier if he were pampered."

Nutmeg's face pushed up against the metal door. "I appreciate the gesture. I'd be way less annoyed if some of your snacks made it into my cell."

Addison huffed. "It's not a cell. You're not in prison. You are so dramatic."

A man passing by gave her the oddest look. She gave him a bright smile. "Dogs, am I right?"

He looked away and rushed toward the back of the plane. Geez, people talked to their pets every day. Although she would admit her talk of incarceration was a bit odd.

The plane door was sealed shut as the flight attendant spoke through the overhead speaker. Addison sat back and watched the safety presentation. It had been a long time since she'd been on a plane. A refresher was never a bad thing.

As they taxied the runway, Luna squealed. As the plane gained speed, she grabbed Xavier's hand and held on with a death grip. Maybe Minnie should have knocked her out for this part.

To his credit, Xavier didn't fight it when Luna ended up hugging on to his arm. He fought back a smile as he quietly talked to her.

They were lucky to have such a good man in their lives. Addison just wished she felt more toward him. Sure, she'd imagined him in bed more than a few times. Her feelings toward him never developed past friendship, though. More than once, he'd melted her heart with his goodness. When she thought about it, she realized she had been so desperate to have a real man in her life that she was forcing there to be romantic feelings where there weren't any.

Her emotional clarity came when she was laying in bed two nights earlier watching *The Wedding Date*, one of her all-time favorite movies, and Dermot Mulroney's character said the panty-melting line, 'I think I'd miss you even if we'd never met'. The depth of the character's connection hit her like a ton of bricks. She hadn't had a love like that in her marriage, and when she thought about Xavier, she realized she had no desire to have a deeper connection with him. He was meant to come into her life and remind her that there were good men in the world and to be a friend right when she needed one.

The seatbelt light made a sound as it was turned off. They'd reached cruising altitude, and she hadn't even noticed. A moan from Nutmeg's carrier had her bending over to look inside. "You okay in there?"

He was on his back, rubbing his belly with his tiny paws. He was obviously miserable, so she resisted smiling and mentioned how adorable he was for like the hundredth time. He opened his eyes and looked up at her. "I thought I hated teleporting with Clarice. This is so much worse."

Minnie popped up in the aisle. "What's going on?"

"Nutmeg has motion sickness. He's not looking so good," Addison replied.

Minnie looked in at him and whispered something before picking up the carrier and moving it to her seat.

Addison gasped. "You're so mean moving him."

Minnie sat in his empty seat and gave her a droll look. "I knocked him out. No way he'd feel any sickness while he was unconscious. And before you ask, yes, I took care of the family. The mother will also have lots of sexy dreams. I wasn't sure what she was into, so I varied what she'll see. If nothing else, she'll get an education."

Addison dropped her head in her hands. "I love you and you're brilliant, but sometimes you take it a bit too far."

Minnie sniffed. "Trust me. She'll wake up refreshed and feeling tingly in all the right places." She turned in her seat to face Addison better. "Now, let's recap our mission while we're in Scotland."

Addison thought back to everything that had

happened in the last two months. She'd discovered so much already, and all of it led to more mysteries. "Well, the first thing we're going to do is visit my family home. I need to learn more about my ancestry. We'll try to meet up with Marilyn and Antony and get an update on their search for my mother. I don't want to leave Scotland without knowing if she is alive or dead."

Minnie reached over and squeezed her hand. "I hope we can find out too, but it's been forty-six years. I don't want you to get your hopes up. It's probably going to take a while to retrace her steps."

Tears welled in Addison's eyes. "I know. I keep telling myself I can't miss her or mourn her if I've never met her. My heart isn't listening to that logic, though."

"No matter what we find out, Xavier, Luna, and I will be by your side. We're the best damn magical friends a girl could have."

Warmth filled Addison. It was the first time Minnie had shown any genuine feelings toward her and she'd never called her a friend before. Was she finally breaking through the barriers her emotional support witch had walled up around her?

Minnie cleared her throat and looked around awkwardly. "And on that weird note, I'm going to take my seat and go have some sexy dreams of my own." She stood up and then turned back. "Do you want me to give you some, too?"

Addison held her hands up and shook her head. "Absolutely not. I'll handle that part myself."

Minnie shrugged, reached over, grabbed Nutmeg's carrier, and put it in the empty seat. "Suit yourself. See you in a couple of hours."

Addison glanced at the carrier. Nutmeg was still on his back, breathing deeply as a string of drool ran down his cheek. She really hoped Minnie hadn't sent him any dreams. What would groundhog porn even look like?

She chuckled and cleared the images from her head. She definitely didn't want to know.

The flight attendant walked by and handed her a blanket and eye mask. This was the good life. She got comfortable and took a deep breath. The sooner she fell asleep, the sooner they'd be in Scotland. Now all she had to do was avoid dreaming about groundhog porn. The image of one on a stripper pole and another with a leather mask on made her shudder. Damn her overactive imagination. There was no chance she was going to have good dreams now.

three

ADDISON RUBBED HER BLEARY EYES. Thanks to an excessive amount of spicy dreams, she didn't sleep well on the plane. The drive to her family home was supposed to only be an hour. She'd like to crash in a bed and sleep for ten hours. The excitement of where she was would likely overrule that once she got there.

Xavier stood at the rental car counter and dropped his head into his hands. Luna was closest, so she offered to check on him. After a few seconds of listening, she burst into laughter and patted his back. She took over working with the agent and came back with keys in hand and a huge smile on her face. "Our boy here apparently can't understand a Scottish accent. They tried three agents and he couldn't understand any of them. I don't know what the problem was. I had no issue."

He glared at her. "They sound like they have marbles in their mouths."

She shrugged as she handed over the keys. "Come on, let's get on the road."

They followed the signs to the pickup area and stopped in their tracks. The only van left in the lot looked like it was made in the seventies and had seen better days.

Minnie crossed her arms in front of her. "Um, what's this?"

"Remember how thrilled you were with those first-class tickets?" Xavier rubbed the back of his neck nervously. "Well, I forgot to reserve a car. There's a big football tournament here this week, so this was literally the last car they had available."

Luna snorted. "Now it makes sense why they were laughing and told us good luck."

Riotous laughter erupted from the pet carrier. "It's nice to not be the one they are mad at. Terrifying isn't it?" Addison sighed as she pulled Nutmeg out of his carrier. The groundhog didn't read a room very well.

The sliding door on the side of the van squealed loudly as Xavier pulled it open. He glanced around the drab brown interior. "It's not that bad. Ignore the cigarette burns in the seats and it's quite charming."

Addison felt so bad for him. He was trying so hard to make the situation better. She patted him on the shoulder as she handed him Nutmeg's carrier to put in the back row. "This is an adventure and we're already starting off with a great story."

The lines around his eyes instantly smoothed out. He mouthed thank you to her.

Minnie cracked her knuckles as she studied the van. "I can do a magickal glow up on this heap."

Addison held her hand up to stop her. "Nope. It's part of the adventure. It'll be good for you to experience a little less perfection and beauty in your life."

Minnie grumbled to herself as she climbed into the middle row.

Luna tossed her suitcase next to Nutmeg's carrier and slid into the seat next to Minnie. "No complaints from me. Let's do this."

Addison climbed onto the passenger side and settled Nutmeg on her lap. "Hey Minnie, can you take the glamor off of him now?"

Luna reached forward and scratched his head. "He's so cute though, with his flat little face."

Nutmeg chittered at her. "I'll have you know I'm considered a ten compared to other groundhogs."

Minnie said the command that changed him back. He stretched and shook out his hair. "I know my thumbs aren't as nice as you humans, but man, am I glad to have them back. I don't know how dogs live that way."

Luna pulled something out of her pocket and handed it forward. "Oh, the agent said the area where we're going is pretty remote, so GPS can be wonky."

Addison grabbed the map from her and unfolded it. "Oh my, I haven't used one of these in twenty years."

Xavier shook his head. "This is going to be so much fun. Hold on to your hats ladies and ground-hog." He turned the key, and it started instantly and immediately backfired loudly. Everyone except Nutmeg jumped. Xavier threw it in reverse. "Hey, it started on the first try. I'm not going to push our luck."

To their relief, the GPS worked perfectly getting them out of town. Even when some roads were barricaded for a football match, it was able to reroute easily. Ten minutes outside of town was another story. All four phones' GPS showed offline.

They pulled over so Addison could get her bearings on where they were on the map. "I feel like Lewis and Clark over here." Her finger ran along the lines crisscrossing the paper. "I think we're here. We have like a pinky length to go to the next road."

Xavier lifted one eyebrow. "Lewis and Clark used fingers as units of measurement?"

"Can you prove they didn't?" She shot back.

"Touche." He pulled back on the road and flipped the switch to the radio. An ear-piercing sound boomed through the van.

"Oh my god. Someone's killing a cow on the radio." Minnie held her hands over her ears.

Addison turned the volume down and tried flipping the station. The dial wouldn't move. "Okay, so it's either silence or bagpipes."

Luna was smiling out the window. "I like it. I vote we keep it on."

There was a grinding sound as the music stopped and a puff of smoke plumed up from the radio. "Absolutely not." Minnie shot back.

Luna threw her hand in the air, pointing at the dashboard. "Geez, you didn't have to fry the radio."

"Oh no," all eyes turned to Xavier as he pulled the van to the side. It rolled to a stop as smoke billowed from under the hood.

"Minnie!" all three yelled at the same time.

She gasped in outrage. "You think I want to spend any more time in this van than we have to? That was not me."

This kept getting better and better. "Hopefully it's something you can fix easily."

Xavier slowly turned toward her. "Me? Hate to break it to you ladies. Just because I'm a man doesn't mean I'm mechanically inclined. That's actually very sexist of all of you." He gave them each a pointed look.

Addison pouted. "I'm sorry. You're right. Anyone have any ideas?"

Luna pointed to a small sticker on the windshield. "They said any problems call that number."

Xavier dialed the number. Thankfully, it was answered immediately. They sat quietly as he relayed their issue and approximate location. He didn't bother with finger measurements.

He was silent for a moment before holding the phone out. "Nothing, I got nothing."

Luna roared as she grabbed the phone. "On behalf of all Americans, I apologize for my friend's hearing issues."

"It can't just be me," He whispered furiously.

Luna listened quietly for a minute. "Sounds

great. We'll hold tight." She handed the phone back to Xavier. "They said they'll send a tow truck in the next two to three hours. All of their drivers are at the football game right now."

"Small-town living is unreal," Minnie grumbled.

A Range Rover drove by, slammed on their brakes, and reversed. The rolled-down window revealed a man who looked very similar to Xavier. "Hey brother, looks like you need some help."

"Skylar, your timing is perfect, like always," Xavier yelled back.

Skylar pulled his car in front of theirs and got out. He looked at the van and then at Xavier. "If you need money, you just have to ask."

Xavier hopped out and hugged his brother. "Haha. I didn't reserve a car, and this was all they had."

"I thought you were traveling with witches? Have them transform it."

"Thank you!" Minnie yelled as she climbed out behind Luna. "I wasn't allowed to. It's part of the adventure."

He nodded in understanding. "I see. So do you want a ride or would that be ruining the adventure?"

All four said ride at the same time.

"Okay, let's get your bags," he paused next to Addison. "Are you holding a groundhog?"

"Yeah, what of it?" Nutmeg shot back.

Skylar held his hands up. "No offense. I wanted to make sure I saw what I thought I saw."

"I appreciate you identifying me correctly. This lot called me every other kind of rodent." Nutmeg sounded genuinely offended. What a faker.

The group piled into the slightly smaller, but significantly nicer SUV. Xavier had the honor of having Nutmeg on his lap since they'd given him the passenger seat.

"Okay, let's see if we can make it to Addison's home without any more problems." Skylar just had to say that, didn't he? He must not know the luck Addison had. If something could go wrong, it would.

four

THE FURTHER THEY DROVE, the more the knot in Addison's stomach grew. She was excited to see her home, but she was also scared and anxious. What would they find when they got there? Would there be any people who knew her mother?

A chill ran down her arms as they crossed a magical barrier. As they drove through it, a large gate appeared on the right side of the road. Skylar pulled up in front of them. "Anyone see a call box or anything?"

A screech rang through the air as the gates opened automatically. Maybe they were spelled to recognize if a family member drove up?

The long, and winding dirt road had no end in

sight. The rolling green hills were breathtaking. Was all of this land really hers?

She did a double take and plastered her forehead to the window. "You guys see that, right?"

Luna was squished against her as Minnie leaned across to look out the window.

Skylar was the first to answer. "I see the trees and the grass. Is that what you mean?"

"No. The man coming toward us." She jabbed her finger at the window, pointing to the right.

"Sorry, I don't see anyone," Xavier said.

"Why are you teasing us?" Minnie asked.

Addison jerked her head around. "What? You guys don't see a large man in a kilt riding his horse straight for us?" Was she losing her mind?

For a few seconds, everyone was silent until they burst into laughter. Even Nutmeg was chittering.

She reached out and smacked Luna and Minnie. "You guys suck. I was starting to think I was losing my mind."

The laughter fell away. It was the wrong choice of words. Something had made her mother go crazy. Who's to say it wasn't hereditary?

Luna squeezed her hand in acknowledgment and changed the subject. "I knew men in Scotland wore kilts. I didn't expect to see one that looked like he rode straight off the cover of a historical romance."

She wasn't exaggerating, either. He had long blond hair, a billowing white shirt, and a green and blue plaid kilt. To get herself hyped for Scotland, Addison had read a few books based in Scotland and this man really looked like he came right out of the book she read called 'The Laird's Promise' by Cassidy K. O'Connor. She never thought she'd actually be living it, though.

The man in question veered to the left and rode ahead. By the time they pulled in front of the ancient-looking castle, he was waiting by the entry.

Minnie whistled as she took in the mansion. "I knew your family was old, but damn, this is next level. And the magick radiating from every corner is almost overwhelming." She reached her hand out as if to caress the magical aura.

Addison wanted to take in the house, but the kilted man was staring intently at her.

"Um Addison," Nutmeg sounded nervous, "I forgot to tell you something."

Before she could question him further, the blonde giant was in front of her. "My elusive fiancée, I was losing hope you'd ever return."

Crazy Scotsman says what?

Her eyes rounded. She couldn't have heard what she thought she had. "I'm sorry, your what?"

His toothy smile didn't falter. "My fiancée." He glanced around at the others. "We've been betrothed since birth. I was starting to think she wouldn't return until we were too old to have children."

Addison choked on air. She didn't know you could do that, but she did. "Okay, I don't know who you are, but you are going to have to rewind quite a bit and catch us all up. Can we go inside first?"

"Of course." Everyone was still awkwardly standing around as he opened the back of the SUV, grabbed four suitcases, and whistled as he walked right up to the front door and inside.

What on earth was happening? She blinked a few times and glared at Nutmeg. "I'm guessing there is a lot you forgot to tell me. We'll talk about that later."

Luna had the gall to walk up and hug her. "You're getting married. That's awesome. I hope I'm a bridesmaid."

"Luna. You can't think this is real? He's either delusional or pulling a prank. I'm not marrying anyone and I'm certainly not having children." Addison glanced at each person. They had a mixture of confusion and humor on their faces. "Come on. We need to hear what this nutball has to say."

The group was silent as they gathered the rest of their stuff from the car and made their way inside.

The front entry was large and opened to a staircase leading up to the next floor. The crazy Scotsman was standing in the middle, talking to an older woman. Her jaw dropped, but she recovered quickly and walked over to them.

She stopped in front of Addison and curtsied. "It's good to know you're alive. I'm Mrs. Allan and after you get settled, you can let me know what food allergies you and your guests have. Nutmeg, good of you to finally bring her home." She gave the groundhog a pointed look and then spun on her heel. "Follow me. I'll show you to your rooms."

"Wow, Minnie is downright friendly compared to this woman," Xavier whispered.

Footsteps rapidly getting closer revealed an old man nearly running down the hall. When he saw Addison, his entire face lit up. "It's true. Our girl is home." He rushed forward and hugged her. With any other stranger, it would have felt awkward. With this man, it felt like home.

He pulled back and cupped her cheek. "The spitting image of your mother, you are. I'd lost hope of your return." He glanced behind her. "Where is your mother?"

Tears welled in her eyes for the woman she'd never met. "We have a lot to catch up on. I've never met her and knew nothing about this place until last month."

Mrs. Allan paused with one foot on the stairs and turned around. Her grumpy facade gone. She looked devastated. "What do you mean? She said she would be gone awhile. We had hoped she'd return before you were due to be born, but we got a note saying she needed to fix things and would come home when she was better." She stepped back and shook her head. "I'll make some tea and scones. Mr. Allan will show you to the dining room. Let's have a seat and catch up on everything."

Mister Hunky Scotsman patted her shoulder gently. "Why don't you take a minute for yourself? I can get the tea."

He was comfortable enough in her house to cook something in the kitchen? Who was this man?

The old man, whom they now knew was Mr. Allan, held his arm out toward a doorway to their right. "The dining room is this way. We'll be right there."

They made their way across the foyer. Addison

paused at the door to see Mr. Allan hugging his wife as she cried softly.

They obviously loved her mother. She actually felt a little jealous. She ducked into the room and grabbed the seat at the end of the long table.

Luna was quietly counting seats. "There's room for twenty. I've never been at a table this big."

It was elegant, clean, and decorated in soft shades of green. The fireplace looked like it hadn't been used in a long time.

The kilted stranger entered from a back door and set down a large tray with the teapot, cups, scones, jam, and what looked like very white butter.

The Allans came in from the entryway. She shooed the stranger away and set about serving everyone. "You can prepare your scones how you like them. There's jam and clotted cream."

Addison glanced at the others. Luna and Minnie looked as confused as she was about what clotted cream was. She watched the men open the baked goods and smear the jam on one side and the white cream on the other. Confident she would not embarrass herself, she followed suit.

Mrs. Allan sat down and pulled out a piece of paper that looked like it had been unfolded many times. "This is the letter we received from your mother. She was seven months pregnant when she told us she needed to get her head on straight and would be back. Two months later, we got this letter."

Addison's hand shook as she took the note. The writing was messy and crooked on the paper. "Was this her normal handwriting?"

The Allans shook their heads. "No, she had beautiful handwriting. We just assumed it was from the stress of having a newborn. It had to be her though, it appeared on the kitchen counter and it was standard practice that letters between the family were spelled so only the family and staff could see the writing."

"Smart," Xavier said, as he passed the note on to Luna.

Addison blew out a breath. "Okay, so you do know about magic. I wasn't sure."

The Allans and the stranger laughed heartily. "Taran's family has been your neighbor and ally for over five hundred years. Molly's family has served your family for even longer. I married Molly when your mom was still a teenager herself." Mr. Allan stated proudly.

So the stranger's name was Taran.

Mrs. Allen sobered. "You said you just found out about this place. Can you tell us what you know?"

Addison nodded. "A few months ago, I started having a lot of accidents. It started with things catching fire, which I could explain. It was when things like enlarging flamingos, and hair color changing on a whim did I realize there was something else going on." She pointed at Xavier. "He found me and explained magick to me. I thought he was nuts. But then I met Luna and Minnie. We found the family grimoire, unlocked a spell cast over the woman I know as my mother, and our neighbor who turned out to be your Addison's best friend, Norma or Marilyn, as we knew her. Not long after Nutmeg arrived, we started learning about all of this." She waved her hands around the room.

Mrs. Allan shook her head. "I've never heard such absurdity. I know every bit of your family's history and something like this has never happened before. We have to find your mother." Panic rose in her voice.

Taran reached over and patted her hand. "My family will, of course, help in any way. Anything you need."

Addison studied his well-chiseled face and perfect jawline. He seemed to genuinely care and if his aura had been off, Luna would have already told her. How were their families connected?

Mr. Allan took one long sip to finish off his tea. "Let's get everyone settled in their rooms. Then we'll give you a tour of the house and after dinner, we can go over all of this again in detail. There's nothing this family can't accomplish. You don't know it yet, but you will be the key to finding your mother."

Great. No pressure or anything.

five

ADDISON WALKED around the large bedroom with a cathedral ceiling and oversized fireplace. Mrs. Allan had explained that her bedroom was still set up like a nursery, so they put her in her mother's room instead.

It was eerie to stand where her mother once had. There wasn't a piece of dust anywhere and fresh flowers were on the bedside table. The Allans had done their jobs well considering having no boss in forty-six years.

She ran her hand across the books lined up alphabetically. Each one was about a different area of magick and right in the middle was a romance novel with a couple embracing on the cover. It actually made her feel closer to her mom knowing she was a normal woman like her.

The desk drawer slid open easily. A journal lay on top of stacks of paper. Her hand itched to grab them and dive in. She wanted to know all of her mother's thoughts. She closed the drawer quietly. Doing that felt like she was admitting her mother was never coming home. Until she had definitive proof, she wouldn't invade her mother's privacy.

A bell rang down the hall. Mrs. Allan had explained it was how the family was called for meals and meetings. There was little technology in the home and it was too huge to shout, so the bell made sense, even if it was a bit outdated.

She opened her door and found Luna, Minnie, and Xavier ahead of her in the hall. Mrs. Allan waited at the top of the stairs. Nutmeg sat on a hall chair talking quietly with her. They hushed when the group caught up to them. That groundhog was hiding more, she just knew he was.

"I hope all of your rooms are to your liking. If there is something you need, let me know. Mr. Skylar said he had other business and would be back for dinner. As for the tour, the other side of the hall has six matching bedrooms to the six on your side. Every bedroom has a private bathroom and there are four bathrooms downstairs." She talked as she walked them past the rooms with all of their doors open. These definitely hadn't had anyone living in them. With their tidy and generic decor, it was obvious these were guest rooms.

She led them down the stairs and through the dining room and kitchen. Everything was outdated. It was as if time had stood still once her mother disappeared. "How are you paying for the upkeep of the house and your salaries? Nothing appears modern. Are you functioning here without the internet?" The idea was absurd. The rest of her group chuckled along with her until they saw Mrs. Allan's face.

She kept a straight face as she looked at each of them. "We live on the property and take in a modest income. It is our honor to serve your family. We have full access to the household accounts and, of course, the vault in case of emergency. We don't leave the property so we are only somewhat familiar with the internet but Taran's family runs errands for us and if a computer is needed for something, they handle it for us. I assure you, we are quite content in our little corner of the world."

The silence was deafening. How was she supposed to respond to something like that? They had stepped back in time. It was one more complication they didn't need.

When it was clear no one knew what to say, she continued walking. Addison's breath was taken when she stepped into the library. Portraits of past Addison's and their families hung on all four walls. There were so many, and every one of them looked remarkably like her. It was like seeing a glimpse of what your life would look like in different realities.

As soon as Addison had free time, she was coming back and studying each picture. She wanted to memorize everything about them, to study the ways they were alike and different.

"Where does this lead?" Minnie's hand was on an ornate door on the back wall. "The magick exuding from here is intense." Addison took her mind off the pictures and focused on the door. Minnie was right. There was power like nothing she'd seen before coming from whatever was behind that door.

Mrs. Allan stepped next to her. "That is Addison's private room. No one can enter except an Addison. Sadly, that means it hasn't been dusted in more than forty years." She shuddered at the thought. Dust bunnies probably ran scared of her.

"You've never seen what's in there?" Luna's eyes sparkled with excitement.

She shook her head. "No one has to my knowledge. I know a few hundred years ago a warlock tried to enter, and the story goes that he instantly turned to ash. I don't want to clean anything that badly."

There was a lot to unpack in that sentence. Addison would save it for another time.

Minnie took a small step away from the door. "It's a good thing we have an Addison with us. Come on, tell us what's in there."

Her hand shook as she reached for the door handle. A tendril of energy reached out and caressed her hand, inviting her to grab the knob and go inside. Emotions she couldn't identify rushed through her. It felt like the air had left her lungs.

"It might be best if Addison goes through that door when she's alone." Taran's sexy brogue rang across the room. Everyone spun around to see him leaning in the doorway with his legs crossed at the ankles and his arms folded. He looked like he didn't have a care in the world.

Addison could see past that. His eyes were on her and they were telling her it was okay to slow down. He was right. She would rather face whatever was behind that door while she was alone. She mouthed a thank you to him. He nodded back at her.

Mrs. Allan cleared her throat. "Right, now let's go see the garden and the stables."

As they passed by Taran, Minnie, and Luna looked back at her and gave her goofy smiles.

She stopped in front of him. "Thank you for that. I was overwhelmed, and you saved me."

"I'll always be here for you." The sexy dimple in his right cheek deepened as he gave her a smoldering look.

Shit. That was a good line. Who was this man and why did he think they were engaged?

He pushed off the wall and gave her a tiny bow. "While the rest of your party is occupied, would you like to take a walk? You can ask me anything you want."

It probably wasn't smart to take off with a man she didn't know. The questions burning inside her outweighed any worries she had. Besides, she was a witch. If he got handsy, she'd turn him into a slug. "Lead the way."

She followed him across the house and out the front door. His horse was still tied to an anchor in the wall. He deftly swung himself into the saddle. His kilt swung enough to give her a tease as to what was underneath. He leaned down and held out his hand. "Let me show you where you're from."

What in the historical romance novel was happening? Minnie and Luna were never going to believe her. Echoes of the past danced on the wind as it pushed her toward him. Every cell in her body was telling her she could trust him.

What the hell. When was the next time a kilted sex god was going to ride up and try to whisk her away?

THE WIND WHIPPED Addison's hair in her face as Taran urged the horse to run. The fear of falling off was enough to distract her from the fact that she was straddled in front of him with her back against his impressively hard chest. Her mom and sons would never believe this happened. Where were Minnie and Luna to take a picture for proof?

The horse deftly climbed a hill and stopped when Taran pulled the reins back. He pointed off to their left. "That house over there is where I live. You can see the small stone barrier between our proper-ties." He pointed to the right. "You have several acres that go along the coastline, but this is what makes our homes so special." In front of them, the deep blue water was churning and crashing against the cliff side. "This is the Moray Firth and beyond that is the North Sea."

Addison hadn't heard that word before. Hopefully, she wasn't turning into Xavier, unable to understand their accents. "What's a firth?"

He tilted his head as he thought, "I believe you would call it an inlet. That doesn't sound very exciting though, does it?"

With the easy question out of the way, it was time to get to the bottom of this engagement mess. "And how are our families connected?"

"We've been neighbors for many generations. The story goes, one of the Addisons became extremely close with my great, great, so many great grandma Adelaine. They were inseparable. Adelaine was being forced to marry a man three times her age and rumored to be a nasty man. Your Addison revealed her magick to Adelaine and offered to help. The story gets murky here. Some say she had the man killed, others say they spelled him and her father to forget the whole arrangement. No one knows for sure. It seemed every unworthy suitor that came calling ended up leaving without a word. Eventually, a man came along that Adelaine wanted, but soon after their wedding, he fell ill. On death's door, Addison did her magick and saved him. Our families have been forever entwined since."

The idea that her relative may have killed men just so her friend didn't have to marry wasn't the greatest family history. She was loyal to her friend though. Addison was going to focus on that and not on the nasty murder business. "That all makes sense. Now, how did we end up engaged?"

A small smile lifted the corner of his mouth. "Our mothers were good friends and pregnant together. Your mother said she had a vision that we were soul mates and would have a love stronger than anything the world had seen before. That was enough for my mom. They agreed on the arranged marriage and I was raised learning everything about both family's histories and, with my mother's insistence that you would return and we would be married. I admit I didn't hold out much hope it would happen. I'm ashamed to say I did date. Is that cheating?"

He looked down at her with a questioning gaze. Was he actually worried about her answer? Wait until he finds out about her past.

She opened and closed her mouth. How did she broach this with him tactfully?

Thankfully, he saved her by throwing back his

head and laughing heartily. "I didn't mean to panic you. All of that is true. However, I'm not ashamed of dating and I know it wasn't cheating. I'm sure you had a life of your own as well."

Her shoulders sagged in relief. "You had me going there for a second. I was actually unhappily married and had three amazing sons. I've been happily divorced for almost two years now and my sons are still amazing." She studied his face, looking for signs of sadness or anger. Instead, he looked interested.

"I hope to meet your sons one day." He reached down, his hand gently lifted her chin toward him. "I'm sorry you were ever unhappy. I promise to be everything you need and want."

The way he accented the word want on top of his brogue made her insides melt. She blinked to clear her head. "Woah there boy." She pulled her chin from his hand. "You are just accepting the betrothal without knowing me? You're fine with it not being your choice?"

He gazed out at the water before answering. "You'll understand one day. The more you become one with this place and accept your family history, you'll understand that your mother wouldn't have gotten that wrong. If she said we are soul mates, I believe it." He let out a heavy breath. "If you decide you don't want to marry me, I won't force you. I'll still protect your family as everyone in my family has done and my children will as well."

Man, they sure did things differently in Scotland. She wasn't sure if it was a cult or not. Did he need to be rescued and deprogrammed from some brainwashing? She had more questions than when they started. "Thank you for understanding. I need time to figure out who I am and then I can think about who we are. I would like to meet your mother, though. I'm sure she has stories she can share with me about my mother."

"Trust me, she's dying to meet you. I promise to do my best to have her tone down her instinct to immediately treat you as her daughter-in-law and start planning the wedding."

Oof. Maybe she'd hold off meeting her potential mother-in-law until she had a better grasp on everything else going on in her life. She didn't need another distraction while she tried to find out if her mother was still alive or not. That was all that mattered right now. That and getting internet as soon as possible. Just because her house looked medieval didn't mean she needed to live in the Dark Ages.

seven

ADDISON SQUARED her shoulders as she entered the dining room. Her friends were going to have so many questions, and they were going to have to wait. Taran would be eating with them. She hadn't intended to invite him. It just slipped out.

Xavier and Skylar stood near the fireplace, deep in conversation. Minnie and Luna were drinking wine at the table. Everyone went silent immediately. All eyes were on them as they walked in. The curiosity burning off her friends was off the charts. She was going to drag dinner out as long as possible to torture them.

Mrs. Allan walked out the door leading from the kitchen, pushing a cart with trays of food. "I went for a simple meal tonight. Roast chicken with neeps and tatties."

Xavier leaned toward Luna. "Is this an accent thing again, or did she say something really weird?"

"I can't help you this time. I'm as clueless as you." She replied as she craned her neck to see what was in the bowls being set on the table.

Addison considered herself an adventurous eater. Neeps and tatties sounded downright scary.

Mrs. Allan paused next to Addison. "Nutmeg said he had some things to do and would be back later."

How mysterious her familiar was being.

Taran grabbed the closest bowl and paused when he saw everyone staring. "Are you not hungry?"

Addison shrugged. "That heavily depends on what neeps and tatties are."

Taran threw his head back and laughed loudly. The sound made her stomach do a flip.

"You have nothing to worry about. It's not like its haggis or blood pudding. I would stay away from those unless you are an adventurous eater. Neeps are creamed radishes and tatties are potatoes."

Xavier and Skylar grabbed the bowls and started

dishing like they hadn't been as worried as they were.

Luna grabbed a roll and passed the basket. "So, Skylar, tell us about the real Xavier. He kind of swooped in and became our knight in shining armor." Addison's eyebrows rose. That was definitely a different tune from when Luna called him 'nothing special'. What had happened while Addison had slept on the plane?

Luna continued, unaware of how confused she'd made Addison and Minnie. Curiously, Xavier was smiling shyly and didn't look surprised at all. Very interesting. "It's pretty brave of him to hang with three witches who seem to find themselves in a lot of trouble. He said his family is magical but has never elaborated."

Skylar studied his brother for a few seconds. "Xavier has always been humble. Xavier is one of seven. You can imagine the hell we put him through while we were growing up and learning how to use our magic." He clapped his brother on the shoulder. "He was one hell of a terror himself. I'm pretty sure he got in more trouble with our parents than anyone else did."

Xavier snorted. "Only because you guys could magically cover up most of the trouble you got into."

"Hey. We covered for you too whenever we could." Skylar shot back.

Xavier chuckled. "That is true. I learned pretty quick to always have one of you nearby."

Addison was impressed. Xavier didn't look jealous or annoyed, and Skylar didn't sound pompous. The brothers seemed to genuinely like each other. Her boys were like that too. She hoped they would always remain that close, even after she was long gone.

"I would love to hear some of the crazy stuff Xavier did." Minnie looked all too happy to collect dirt on him to mock him with later.

"Miss." Mr. Allan came into the room holding a small metal box. Whatever was inside was shrieking. "The wards don't allow anyone except family to portal onto the property. This woman tried a few times and ended up at the outside gate screeching your name. She was so angry over her magick not getting her in that she didn't even notice me coming behind her and putting her in this iron box."

What now? Couldn't they have a few hours of normalcy?

Mr. Allan set the box at the end of the table. Everyone gathered around as Addison reached forward and opened the lid. A tiny, bright light shot into the air and instantly spewed swear words.

"How dare you put me in there. Iron hurts, damn it." She flew into Mr. Allan's face and poked his nose. "You didn't even try to keep the box steady while you walked. I bounced around like a ping-pong."

"Clarice? What are you doing here?" The tiny fae had looked better. Her hair was a mess, and she had red patches of skin all over her body. Did iron burn fairies?

The indignant fairy flew over and bobbed in front of Addison. "I missed my friends. Isn't that a valid reason to come visit?"

There was no way she was telling the truth. "Try again."

"Fine. My entire realm is up in arms since I sent Malachi there without permission. He was causing a lot of headaches. I was sent away until I found somewhere to send him that was far from our realm."

Ugh. She had hoped the dark wizard was out of their lives for good. If the fae couldn't handle him, what made them think anyone else could?

Clarice glanced at the table. Her eyes lit up as she flew straight at the bowl of potatoes.

"Sure, help yourself," Addison muttered as she went back to her seat.

She gave the fae a few minutes to eat her fill before interrupting her. "So, what are you going to do with him?"

Clarice shrugged as she wiped butter off her face. "I'm working on that. I'll let you know when it's figured out."

Addison didn't like the sound of that. Then again, Malachi wasn't the fae's problem to begin with. Maybe she could reach out to the secret magickal society she was now a part of. They handled the rogue witches well when they were spelling shifters to do their dirty work. Clarice would have to stick around until Addison had a chance to talk to the group. "Why don't you stay the night? We apparently have a lot of empty rooms available."

"Well, if you insist." She shook her tiny body, and suddenly her hair was perfect again and her skin was healed. Did Addison just get scammed?

One thing was certain, she hadn't had a dull day since learning she was a witch.

Clarice pointed over her shoulder at Taran. "Who's the hunk?"

"I'm engaged to Addison." He beamed proudly.

Clarice looked ready to explode with questions. Addison glared at her and shook her head.

For once, the fae seemed to get it and went back to eating.

Lovely. Another person who was going to badger Addison for answers she didn't have. She really needed to find her mother alive. She had a lot of questions for her. Starting with, 'Why the hell did you betroth your unborn daughter?'. This wasn't the eighteen hundreds. It wasn't like they were offering a cow for payment. The old days were unreal.

eight

IT TURNED out that waiting for a house full of people to fall asleep was boring. It was after midnight when the boys had finally gone off to bed. Addison wanted to be completely alone and undisturbed when she went back to the portrait room and the secret door.

She slipped into the library and locked the door behind her. She leaned against the door and quieted her mind while she scanned the paintings again. There was so much history she knew nothing about. When she looked at other boys in the portraits, she could see glimpses of her sons. It still wasn't real to see so many doppelgangers of herself. She made her way around the room, taking in as many details as she could. When she made it to the last painting, she pulled a chair in front of it and sat. Staring back at her were her grandparents and her mother when she was a teenager.

She was beautiful. Was she happy? Did she like being a witch? Why did she abandon her newborn child? Who was her father?

The blue eyes staring back at her didn't give her any answers. She took a picture of the painting and texted it to the boys with the message, 'Meet your grandmother and great grandparents'. She could only imagine what they were thinking about all of this.

With the portraits not giving her any information, she turned her attention to the secret door. Excitement coursed through her. There was going to be a treasure trove of answers in there. There had to be.

Her hand shook as she reached for the handle. The image of her turning to ash gave her pause. Did she trust all of this was real? Was she really an Addison and would be allowed inside? There was only one way to find out.

The ornate wooden door swung open silently. There was no whoosh of magick or loud creaking of an ancient door that hadn't been opened in forty years.

There was a slight musty smell, likely from being unused for so long, mixed with the scent of incense and ash. Flames flickered to life in small lanterns, illuminating a short hallway leading to a large archway. The wall the door had been on was an exterior, so logically there should be no space for any of this. One thing was certain, magick wasn't logical.

Through the opening, a large room was illuminated when more lanterns lit on their own. The cavernous room looked exactly like you would expect a witch's workroom to look like. There was an altar along one wall. Shelves were filled with bottles and jars of different sizes, full of who knew what. Along another wall was a desk covered with papers and books. She was even surprised to see a small bed tucked into one corner. She could see how she could lose track of time in there and need a quick nap.

None of this was strange. What was odd were the symbols drawn in ash around the room and even on the floor. The lines looked ragged, as if done with an unsteady hand. These were much different from the ones the rogue witches had been using.

It was going to take everyone's help to research these. She walked around and took pictures of each one. Above the altar was a drawing of a person's outline surrounded by a golden light with a few symbols drawn underneath.

How was she possibly going to catch up with forty-six years of missed teaching? There was so much she didn't know. Was it possible to learn everything she needed to?

On the altar was a single sheet of paper. On it was a message written in the same chaotic handwriting of the note her mother had sent the Allans.

'

If you are reading this, it means my baby survived. I'm sorry for leaving you. I had to hide you.
Don't trust the Addisons.'

She flipped the paper over and back again. There was nothing else. "What the hell? That's all you leave me? You couldn't spell this out a little better? Who drops a bombshell like that without more context?" She knew her mother couldn't hear her. It didn't matter. She needed to voice her frustration. She tossed the paper down. "No. There has to be more."

She wasn't leaving this room until she found at

least one answer to any of the hundred mysteries she was dealing with. "Okay Mom, show me something."

Addison jerked awake as her phone rang loudly. Luna's face was on the screen. "Hello?"

"Finally. Are you in your secret room? We've been looking for you and that's the only place we haven't checked."

Addison glanced around. She had fallen asleep at some point while reading one of the many books in there. At least she'd made it to the bed. "Yeah, sorry. I guess I fell asleep in here. I'll be right out."

She stood up and moaned as a wave of dizziness hit her. Her sleep hadn't been peaceful. It felt like someone had been banging a drum in her head for hours. When was the last time she'd woken up with a headache?

She grabbed the note off the altar and made her way back to the library. Her entourage, including Taran, was standing on the other side of the door waiting for her. Luna had a cup of coffee and a scone ready to go.

She took them gratefully. "Sorry guys, I didn't mean to disappear on anyone."

"Well, spit it out? What's in there?" Minnie was practically bouncing on her toes she was so excited. The witch was a serious nerd for all things magick.

"Give her a minute to eat," Taran interjected. It felt kind of good having someone look after her.

Minnie didn't argue. She huffed and plopped down on a couch. She had no understanding of how raw and emotional all of this was for Addison. This wasn't a fun adventure for her.

When she felt more in control, she set down the coffee cup and pulled out the note she'd stuffed in her pocket. As each of them passed the message around, she recounted everything she saw inside. By the time it made it back to her, everyone looked at her with pity. Even Minnie. Maybe she was getting it.

"I haven't been through everything yet, but I couldn't find any reference as to which Addison I couldn't trust and why." What was her mother so scared of? "I need a shower. Xavier, can you work with Taran to get an internet service installed? We're going to need it. I'm going to text you all the pictures I took inside there. Can you do some research and see if you can identify any of them?"

Luna still looked like she wanted to cry for Addison. "Of course. Take your time showering. We'll set up a research area and have all the laptops ready to go when there is internet. In the meantime, we'll do the best we can on our phones."

When all this was over, Addison was going to have to find a way to thank all of them for staying by her side. She never had close friends and her husband was far from what anyone would call a supportive partner. It felt odd to not have to do everything on her own. Everyone needed people they could lean on, and boy was Addison going to need them. She had a feeling the craziness was just getting started.

nine

ADDISON HAD two missed calls and a text message from her son, Leo.

> Leo: We talked to the necromancer. She has a friend who can portal all of us to you at 3 o'clock your time. Does this work?

Addison's son was in love with a ghost. Like a real Casper-type ghost. Francesca was beautiful and sweet and died in the 1920s. Addison hadn't wanted to encourage the relationship because there was no happy ending for them. Then they found out about a necromancer who could put a ghost's spirit inside a recently deceased body and they would have a second chance at life. It sounded insane to her, but with everything she'd seen in the last few months, it was obvious the impossible could actually be possible. She had insisted on meeting the necromancer before they did anything. Francesca may be a ghost, but she was still a person. Maybe it was the mom in her. She wasn't going to let anyone harm her son's translucent girlfriend.

> Addison: We can make that work.
> There's a ward around the house so
> they can't portal here. We'll meet
> you at the gate.

She didn't know how portaling worked. She had to hope they had some kind of magickal GPS or something to pinpoint their landing zone.

It was almost noon. They could get a few hours of research in before their guests arrived. She knew nothing of necromancers, so that would be a good place to start.

Addison leaned against the hood of Skylar's Range Rover and stared at the empty road behind the wrought-iron gate. Her guests would arrive any minute. At five minutes after three, there was a whoosh of air as a swirl of color appeared on the side of the road and Leo walked out with two women and an impressively large man. A second later, Francesca's faint outline came into view.

The gate opened silently to allow the foursome to enter. She glanced around, expecting to see Mr. Allan nearby with a clicker in his hand. He was nowhere to be seen. Maybe the gate just knew they were allowed inside. Crazier things have happened.

"Mom, this is Ava, her husband Drew, and Olivia. She's the one who portaled us here." His eyes twinkled with excitement.

Addison held out her hand and shook each of theirs. "It's nice to meet you. I'm a little surprised you are here so quickly."

Ava pointed at Olivia. "This one is a romantic. She overheard me talking with your son and insisted we help him immediately. I get the urgency to be with your soulmate once you've found them." She squeezed her husband's hand. The look on his face spoke volumes about how much he loved her. For the first time in her life, Addison was a little jealous. No one had ever looked at her that way before.

An image of Taran popped into her mind. Okay,

so maybe he would look at her one day like that. Would she be around long enough for that to happen? Did she even want to be there? "Let's get up to the house, meet my crew, and then get started."

The out-of-town guests piled into the back seat while Leo hopped in the passenger seat. Francesca was hovering further ahead. She could only go so far from the object she was tied to. In her case, it was a cigarette holder Leo had in his pocket.

The drive was quick and no kilted strangers rode up on them. She led them through the entryway to what Mrs. Allan called the drawing room. She'd already set out tea and scones.

Luna stood by the door, ready to pounce. Addison introduced each person and let Luna chat their ears off as they got their drink and food. Poor Leo and Francesca stood near the window, waiting patiently for everyone to get settled. She could see the stress lines. They were scared, and Addison didn't blame them. She'd done some research already and found no record of a ghost ever being put into a new body before.

Ava set her teacup down and took control of the conversation. "This is not a service I provide and I don't want it to get around that this is a possibility. The last thing I need is a line of ghosts at my house, begging for bodies." Olivia and Drew nodded their agreement. It must suck to have a rare power that everyone wanted a piece of.

Ava continued, "I want to make it clear I've only done this a couple of times. Luckily, both were successful. I can't make any promises, but if you still want to move forward, I'm willing to help."

Leo nodded eagerly. "Absolutely. We won't hold you accountable if anything goes wrong and we won't tell anyone about this."

Addison held up her hand. "Hang on, I want details. No offense to you, Ava, but we don't know you. I want to make sure someone is looking out for Francesca."

A commotion at the door interrupted them as Clarice came flying in. She zeroed in on Olivia and flew straight at her. "I knew I smelled another fae. Did they send you to check up on me? I'm handling Malachi."

"They come in different sizes?" Taran whispered to no one.

Everyone shrugged. The fae were notoriously secretive.

Clarice squinted her eyes. "Oh wait, you're... I'm so sorry. Please forgive me. I promise I'm doing as I was told." She turned around and looked at Addison's group. "Why aren't you all bowing?"

Now Addison was really confused.

"It's okay. Truly." Olivia's cheeks were pink. "Please don't treat me any differently than you would have five minutes ago. I promise I'm no one of importance."

Clarice tsked. "Fae royalty are important."

Olivia rubbed her eyes. "You are correct. I'll make sure the court knows you are doing your job admirably."

Clarice's eyes sparkled as she bowed again and flew out of the room.

The room was silent as all eyes were on Olivia. She finally sighed. "Let's pretend that never happened. We're here for love. Let's do this."

Addison had so many questions. Olivia didn't look like she was going to give up any more information.

"Anyway," Ava looked directly at Francesca. "You will need to find a newly deceased body you are happy with. It'll be your body for the rest of your new life, so choose carefully. It's best to find someone far from where you will live and preferably with few relatives, so you don't have to worry about running into them. Good so far?"

She waited for everyone to nod. "Call when you're ready and we'll either portal to you or bring you to us. We have a very chaotic life, so we could be anywhere when you call."

"Could be Italy, could be Hell," Drew interjected.

Four heads snapped toward him. Did he just say Hell? Like with a capital H? Who were these people?

Ava chuckled when she saw their faces. "I can't imagine what you all are thinking about us right now. I promise we're very sane and mostly normal people." She turned back to Francesca and Leo. "Once I've put Francesca in the new body, I'll tie her life force to yours. I'll give you a pendant you should wear at all times. It will help keep you connected. So far, we've not had to do any maintenance on the connections we've already done, but we'll reach out to you if that changes. This is new magick for all of us. There are no protocols or history to look back on. Now that you know all that, do you still want to proceed?"

Leo and Francesca looked at Addison. The question was clear in their eyes. They wanted her blessing. She glanced at Luna, then Minnie, then Xavier, and Skylar. All four of them knew more about the magical world than she did. Thankfully, she didn't have to voice her question. Each nodded their head.

"Well, okay. If you are good with the risks, you should do it. Francesca deserves a long and happy life. She makes my son happy and if this is what he wants, then I want it to."

It was sad to watch the young couple turn to embrace each other and remember they couldn't. Hopefully, that wouldn't be an issue much longer.

ten

ADDISON STARED out the window of the library while the rest of her group typed away on their computers. They'd had a nice dinner with Ava and her entourage and then drove them to the gate so Olivia could portal them away.

After that, they hunkered down and began the search for what the symbols meant. Addison was having trouble concentrating, though. Nutmeg still hadn't returned, and she hadn't heard a word from him. He was a significantly older being than her, so she tried not to worry. The mother in her knew something was amiss. Luna had tried a locator spell on him, but it didn't work. That was when she'd really lost focus.

Where was her wayward familiar?

Minnie stood and stretched her back. "I'm not through all of my symbols yet, but there is an obvious pattern emerging. These are various runes of protection. Honestly, I'm shocked anyone except the caster was able to go into that room."

Xavier pushed his laptop back. "Same here."

Luna had asked if she could continue translating the grimoire. She rubbed her eyes. "I'm still stuck on the note. If it was your mom who wrote the letter, why was she warning you about other Addison's? And we know from Nutmeg there can only be three Addison's alive at a time. If you and your aunt are accounted for, it must mean your mom is alive, right?"

"You got your facts wrong." Mrs. Allan interrupted as she rolled in a cart with what smelled like coffee. Thank goodness. Tea was great and all but Addison needed the java. "I don't know anything about only three Addisons at a time, but two aunts are alive. Nasty ones they are. They were perfectly fine until your mom got pregnant. Your mom never told anyone who your father was. I assume that's why your aunts were so angry. They must have wanted her to marry before having you. Each time they came around, your mom would get more and more upset. Now that I know she was out of her mind when she gave you up, I can look back and realize the signs were there. I assumed it was pregnancy hormones. I should have kept a better eye on her and I'll regret it for the rest of my days."

Addison's heart dropped into her stomach. If there were two aunts plus her, then how could her mother be alive? "Talk this through with me. My mom shouldn't have even been able to get pregnant with me until one of the aunts died. Medically, there were four of us alive at once, right?"

Xavier blew out a breath. "This is one of the reasons I was never jealous of not having magick. It is so damn complicated."

It was the first time he'd ever mentioned his lack of magick. He truly didn't look bothered.

"Why is it the more we learn, the more questions we have?" Luna growled. "I know the note said not to trust the Addisons, but maybe we should talk to your aunts and at least ask them some questions. We don't have to mention the warning."

"I don't think you'll have to go far." Mrs. Allan stood staring up at the portrait of Addison's mother. "I'm sure they've found out you're here, and I expect they'll show up sooner rather than later. I, for one, can't wait to see their faces when they realize what a beautiful and amazing woman you grew up to be."

"You really think they were that traditional that they were mad my mother was having me out of wedlock?" That just didn't feel right to Addison. There had to be more to it than that.

"I can't say for sure. I haven't seen them in many years. The first few years after your mother's disappearance, they would come around and close themselves up in here. Eventually, the visits stopped and we've not heard a peep out of them since."

Nutmeg said he used to be with a Great Aunt Addison. He had to know more. If he wasn't home by morning, she was going to do some serious magick to find his butt and make him answer some questions.

Luna covered her face, trying to hide a big yawn. "I'm sorry. Between jet lag and staring at a book for hours. I'm exhausted. I'm going to turn in. I promise I'll be right back at this in the morning."

Addison realized she was a terrible friend. "I'm sorry guys. You really don't have to give up all your time to deal with my family drama. You've never been to Scotland before. Tomorrow you should take the day and go sightseeing." Luna and Xavier opened their mouths to argue. "If I find anything out, I will text you guys immediately. And Xavier, you need to spend some time with your brother.

Now, go get some sleep and go be tourists tomorrow."

Minnie didn't have to be told twice. She shut the lid of her computer, blew Addison a kiss, and left.

Mrs. Allan was the last to leave. She gave Addison a pointed stare. "Don't stay up too late. All of this will still be here in the morning."

She was right. That didn't make it any easier to stop. She was close to something. She could feel it deep inside. What secrets were the Addison's hiding?

Addison ran her fingers along the wildflowers as she walked through the open field. The air was cool and smelled of salt water. She bent and plucked a thistle from the ground as a booming sound echoed around her. With each bang, her head felt like it was going to explode. She fell to her knees, her head in her hands. Her eyes burned as the air in front of her shimmered. A man appeared at the same moment the noise and the pain stopped.

He smiled down at her. His aura shining gold was so bright she had to squint to look at him. His hand extended to help her stand. "My daughter, finally we meet."

Crazy glowing daddy says what?

"Could you repeat that?" She couldn't possibly have heard right.

The field morphed, and they were sitting on the couch in the library. "What the hell?"

"Relax. You're fine." He pointed behind her to where her body was slumped over the table. Drool ran out of her mouth onto the book she'd passed out on.

That's what she looked like when she slept?

"You're fast asleep and in no danger from me. I apologize for the pain my arrival caused. During your last sleep, I spent hours trying to get into your mind to talk to you. You're a stubborn one, though." He smiled like he was proud of her fault.

She rubbed her eyes and then stared at her hands. If she was in a dream, how could she feel that? Focus. That was a question for another time. "I'm going to need you to back way the hell up and start at the beginning."

His eyes twinkled. "Are you sure that's what you want? That means going back a thousand years. Are you ready for that much information?"

"That sounds kind of daunting, actually." She

shook her head. "Yes, damn it, I feel like I'm in the center of a tornado being spun in ten different directions."

"Just as fierce as your mother." The love was clear in his eyes.

This couldn't be real. She leaned back and crossed her arms. "So, are you some kind of wizard?"

The smile fell from his face. "Absolutely not." He actually looked disgusted. "My name is Adathan and I'm an angel."

Her jaw dropped and then she leaned forward and belly laughed, harder than she had in years. The absurdity.

He waited for her to quiet down. She mumbled an apology and waved at him to continue.

"Your ancestor, the first Addison, was a low-level witch. One day she prayed for a miracle. Her best friend was being sold to a cruel man, and she wanted to stop it. I'm a guardian angel, so of course I went to her and listened to her plea. I went to look for myself and saw what a despicable man he was. I gave your mother a book. It had everything she needed to stop the wedding on her own. I also gave her a single drop of my power. It would give her an extra boost while she cast to ensure her friend's safety."

His face darkened. "I made two mistakes that day. The book I gave was too powerful, and giving her a taste of my power poisoned her mind. I didn't know it at the time, though. A few weeks after my visit with her, she prayed for me to come to her so she could thank me for saving her friend. When I appeared in that room right over there," he pointed at the ornate door that led to the Addison room. "Manipulating the spells in the book I gave her. She was clever enough to set a trap for me."

Addison's stomach twisted, knowing what was coming next.

"As the binds of magic encircled me, I saw the crazed look in her eyes. She was drunk on power. One of the binds encircled my throat and squeezed, so I struggled to speak. She drew a mark in blood on my forehead and then on hers and said a spell. I watched as a translucent cord extended from me to her. She illuminated when my angel power entered her. I had hoped it would be too much, and she'd die right there. As the magical wall was closing in on me-"

Addison jerked awake. A piece of paper stuck to her cheek thanks to the puddle of drool she'd created. "No. He wasn't finished."

Taran stood over her. It wasn't mortifying at all

when he reached down and pulled the paper off her face. "Are you okay? I was worried you'd been like this all night. I thought maybe I could move you to the couch without waking you up."

Her head still pounded as if Adathan was still in there, knocking on her brain. "I think I just met my father." Taran glanced left and right. She rolled her eyes at him. "I don't mean right now. He came to me in a dream."

Taran's face softened. "I know you want to find your parents. Drudging all this up probably puts all kinds of ideas into your subconscious."

"No. This wasn't a fantasy. He told me the same story you did about the first Addison, but he explained how she did it. She trapped him. I don't know if he's still in there. Let me get the others, so I don't have to repeat this a bunch of times."

He grabbed her arm when she stood up. "They left an hour ago for Edinburgh. Luna told me to tell you 'They were going to tour a real-life freaking castle and would be back soon'."

Yeah, that sounded exactly like Luna. "You didn't quite put the excitement into it she probably did. Want to try that again?"

He cocked an eyebrow. "I don't think it's

possible to match her enthusiasm. Do you want to call them?"

If she told them the story, would they try to turn around and come back? She didn't want to ruin their day, and it wasn't like Adathan told her anything actionable. On her own, she didn't have enough experience to rescue him if he was still in there. Maybe there was a book that talked about imprisoning angels and how to undo it. As if she'd be that lucky. "No. it's okay. I have research I can do until they return. I'll fill you in while I grab breakfast."

"How about this, you can wait to tell me the story until everyone is together?"

"You could wait? The curiosity isn't going to bother you all day?" She would never be able to wait.

"Someone that waits 46 years for something is a very patient person." He winked at her. "Yes, I want to know. I can wait though, I'm a big boy. I can handle the suspense."

He glanced at the table. "It looks like I'm yours for the day. What can I do to help?"

It may have been her imagination, but it sounded like he emphasized the words I'm yours. Did her mother's vision show he was going to be such a gorgeous hunk? His emerald green eyes sparkled back at her like he knew what she was thinking.

The door to the library banged against the wall. Nutmeg bolted in and climbed onto the table. His normally pristine clothes were dirty and singed in some places. "Oh boy, I have a lot to tell you-."

She glared at him. "Yeah, you do. I think there's a lot about my family you didn't tell me."

He held up his tiny paws. "No, you got it all wrong. My memories were manipulated. My wife's too. Now I need your help rescuing her from the rejected familiar realm."

That was a lot to unpack. Where did she even start? "You didn't remember you had a wife?"

He shook his head. "Can you believe that! Your freaking aunts are evil."

There it was again, another red flag about the other Addisons. Now she really wanted to meet them. If they could change a familiars memory, they were definitely juiced up with Adathan's power. She was going to have to be very careful when they were around.

Nutmeg wobbled on his feet.

"When was the last time you slept or ate?" She really should have checked up on him sooner. She was too wrapped up in her own drama.

Taran stood up. "Let me get some food for both of you. You can talk while you eat."

She nodded her thanks and turned back to her distraught familiar. "So, how did you get your memories back?"

"I'm not exactly sure about that part. I was exploring the house when I heard my name whispered. I assumed it was a ghost, but it never revealed itself. I was walking around the ritual site in the woods when the voice got louder. The veil between this realm and the one where familiars live when not bonded to a witch is thin there because of the magic that has been practiced there for hundreds of years."

Taran came back in with a plate of muffins, a mug of coffee, and a glass of orange juice. He didn't interrupt as he set the food down and sat back to let Nutmeg continue.

After a few minutes of chewing, Nutmeg started again. "I slipped into my realm and was surrounded by friends. They fired questions at me and it didn't take long to realize something was really wrong." He paused to take a few more bites of food.

Addison was always a curious person. Sometimes things just stuck in her mind and she needed to know more. She couldn't resist asking. "So, in your realm, do you have houses like we do? I'm trying to picture all types of animals living together in like a neighborhood."

"Focus Addison," It sounded weird to be admonished by a groundhog. "It took a long time to figure out what was going on. Thanks for checking on me by the way. Next time I disappear for almost two days maybe look for me."

He was right. She had no excuse. "I'm sorry."

"I was a familiar for your aunt like I told you. What I didn't remember was that I had a wife and she was a familiar to your other Aunt. The last definite memory I have is coming here to see your mom while she was pregnant with you. My next memory is being called to you. My friends said my wife, Sasha, and I were sent to the rejected familiars realm."

The fear was palpable. How terrible was this rejected familiar place?

"I realized the voice calling to me was Sashas. I don't remember her but I knew I had to see if she was still there. Everyone banded together and searched for a way to find an entrance to the realm. We finally found someone who knew the way. Unfortunately, it was a well-protected portal. You couldn't just enter if you wanted to and it was a one way door. I tried everything to get in. As soon as I got near electricity would zap me."

That explained why his clothes looked like they'd been burned. "I'm so sorry. What can I do to help?"

"We need to find a way in and rescue her. Then we need to confront your aunts." Anger tinged his voice.

"I need to catch you up on what I found out before we do anything. I think the aunts are dangerous and we'll have to be smart when we confront them." If they have angel power and can manipulate powerful familiars than they are not to be underestimated. Everyone had a crazy aunt or uncle in the family but Addison had to get two and their craziness was off the charts.

eleven

ADDISON WAS PACING the hall by the time Luna, Minnie, Xavier, and Skylar walked in. Luna was a giant walking ad for Scotland. From head to toe, she had something with the Scottish flag on it. A stalk of Heather was protruding from her ponytail and she had a stuffed hairy cow under her arm. "Wow, someone had a good time."

Minnie scoffed. "You should have seen the stuff we made her put back. It's these twos' fault. They were so entertained by her childlike joy that they kept offering to pay for stuff." She side-eyed them. "Must be nice to have money to throw around."

Skylar gave her a pointed look. "You weren't complaining when we bought every pastry at every bakery you made us stop at."

"That's beside the point." She wiped her mouth absently.

Luna held up the stuffed animal. "Isn't he adorable? They call them Highland Cow's but with their accent, it sounds like Highland Coo." She gasped. "I almost forgot." She pulled something out of her pocket and handed it to Addison. "Clarice left this morning. She said for you to take care of that and she was sorry."

In her hand was a small metal pink flamingo keychain. "Is she being cute because of the flamingo I blew up? Why would I want this and why do I need to take care of it?"

Luna reached out and snatched it from her. "I'll hold on to it if you want." Everyone stared at her in surprise. "I can't explain it, but I have a connection to it. As soon as I handed it to you, I felt an ache deep inside."

Between Clarice's message and Luna's attachment, Addison had a bad feeling. Why not add it to the long list of other potential disasters they were dealing with? "I'd love it if you hold on to it. Now, I have a lot to catch you up on."

She led the group back to the library where Taran and Nutmeg had been all day helping her look through every book to find any mention of trapping an angel. Spoiler alert, they didn't.

Addison waited patiently while the group recounted everything they'd told her, and Luna showed off all her souvenirs. Finally, everyone was seated and waiting.

"So, I met a man who says he's my father and that he's an angel."

Everyone spoke at once.

"Way to bury the lead." Minnie snarked.

Luna gasped. "Holy crap, why didn't you call us right away?"

Xavier's forehead was scrunched like he was concerned. "And you believe him? No one's ever met an actual angel before, so that would be a pretty incredible story if true."

Addison held her hands up to slow them all down. "And Nutmeg is married and had his memories erased."

All heads swung toward the groundhog, who still looked like he had singed hair in some places.

Luna slapped the table. "We weren't gone that long. No more sightseeing. Start at the beginning."

Addison recounted everything from her dream, the little information they'd found since then, and everything Nutmeg had been through.

Luna's jaw had hung open through the retelling. "Holy crap. This is heavy. How are you both doing?"

How was Addison doing? She'd been so focused on looking for answers, she hadn't taken a second to process her feelings. Now wasn't the time for it, either. "There's a lot to unpack, but I have a feeling there is going to be a lot more. I'm going to compartmentalize until this is over. The question is, what do we do first, confront the aunts, try to free Adathan, or try to rescue Sasha?"

Mrs. Allan knocked gently at the door. "That's a decision better made on a full stomach. Dinner is ready."

Addison rubbed her stomach. "The food here is so much richer. Thank god I'm not lactose intolerant or eating would be a very uncomfortable affair."

Everything seemed to be made with heavy cream. It was definitely more delicious. The calories had to be off the charts, though.

Luna scraped the last bits of chocolate pudding from her bowl. "I'm planning to bribe Mrs. Allan to come home with me."

"She'd probably love to see America. It's too bad

they never will." Taran said casually while he finished his own dessert.

"Why? Is she afraid to travel?" Luna sounded genuinely sad at the thought.

He looked up and realized everyone was staring at him. "Oh, well, I thought you knew. They are elves. They belong to your family. They are tied to the house and can't leave it."

Addison's jaw dropped. "Are you serious? That's awful. Why would we imprison them here?"

Skylar answered for him. "It's very common for magickal families to own elves. Our family no longer does. When Xavier was old enough to figure out they weren't free, he made my parent's lives hell until they agreed to let them go. The elves loved us kids, though, so they stayed on and my parents paid them for their service."

"Awe." Luna's eyes watered as she looked at Xavier. "That was so sweet of you."

Xavier blushed at the praise.

Addison looked at Minnie. "Did you know they were elves?"

She shrugged. "Yes. My family wasn't rich enough to have any. One look at this house and I knew they were. If you opened your senses like I told you, you would have known they were super-natural."

"I've never met an elf before. I didn't realize they look exactly like us," Luna said.

She had never known her family and grew up in the system. Everything she'd learned about magick was done on the streets. For her to have worked hard enough to open her store was always amazing to Addison. It wasn't a surprise she didn't know about this practice that seemed to only be done in the elitist class.

"They don't really look like us. They are spelled to look that way so they can blend in." Minnie replied.

Addison's eyes bulged. "So they can't leave this place and they can't look like themselves. That is bullshit. We need to add that to the list of things we have to handle while we're here."

She was getting a headache thinking about how long their to-do list had become. What started as a singular focus to find her mom had morphed into so much more.

The subject of their conversation walked in and paused when she saw everyone staring at her with a mixture of emotions on their faces.

Addison hopped up and ran over to hug the

older woman. "On behalf of my entire family, I'm so sorry for how we treated you."

Mrs. Allan tilted her head to look at the rest of the group. "Who told her?"

The room was silent. Addison pulled back. "Why didn't you want me to know?"

"You grew up in America with no knowledge of this world. I assumed we would need to slowly teach you all the customs and rules." When she saw how upset Addison was, she cupped her face. "Your family isn't cruel. This is the way it's always been. I was raised learning what I needed so I could be the best caretaker possible."

This was all too much. Addison felt like they were back in the 1800s or something. "But you don't even get to look like yourself."

Mrs. Allan stepped back and shrunk to her normal height of three feet. "I do look the same, just a bit taller. It's very hard to do this job at our natural size."

Addison shook her head. "Well, I'm putting a stop to this. Xavier found a way to break the bond with his family elf and I will too."

Mrs. Allan looked horrified. "Please don't do that. We love it here. We love taking care of you.

Please don't send us away." Tears streamed down her face.

"Addison," Skylar called out. "This is all they know. You are moving too fast. We can take care of this. We just need to slow down a bit and talk it through with them."

She would never have imagined being told you are free would be upsetting. She could see if all they knew was her house, the idea of leaving and losing their purpose would be scary. "I'm sorry. I didn't mean to upset you. Let's worry about it another day. If you are happy, then I am too."

Mrs. Allan nodded her head and went back through the door to the kitchen.

That conversation had really gotten away from Addison. There couldn't possibly be any more surprises, right?

twelve

ADDISON STARED up at the ceiling in the secret ritual room and counted the cracks in the stone. She had been antsy to talk with Adathan in her sleep and didn't know if it would work in her bedroom or if she needed to be in the same place as before. She'd said goodnight to her friends and shut herself in the room.

The picture of the glowing human outline on the wall made a little more sense. It must have represented Adathan and had something to do with the trap he was in. She'd brushed her hand along the wall and reached out with her senses. There was nothing. No hum, no light, no energy. Was he really back there, or had she dreamed the whole thing?

She'd been lying there for the last hour trying to

fall asleep. She needed to know if he was a figment of her imagination or not. Of course, that meant she was wide awake.

All the usual tricks of counting backward from 100 and chanting the word sleep in her head hadn't worked. What she wouldn't give for Minnie to knock her out.

Eventually, she managed to drift off. The now familiar pounding only lasted a few seconds before Adathan appeared and they were back on the couch in the library.

"My beautiful daughter." Ugh, that still sounded so weird to Addison. "I've been waiting for you. I expected you to nap today so we could talk again."

"Trust me, I wanted to. There's a lot going on that is as urgent as your situation. I'm trying to balance it all. I need you to finish your story. We need more to go on."

He seemed mildly put out that she didn't put him above everything else. Sorry buddy, you're new and not in life-threatening danger.

"Back to my story. As the walls were sealing around me, I managed to whisper a promise. Your mother told me you would call it a prophecy."

You will reincarnate forever and have multiple Addisons per generation and the generation that has four Addisons will be the one to free me.

"I've waited many of your human lifetimes with no end in sight. One day, I heard a voice in my head. It was a woman praying for a beautiful family of her own. One that would love her unconditionally and would go to the ends of the Earth for each other. It was the first voice I'd heard since the binding. I tried using my magic again without fail. Suddenly I could feel a mind nearby I could slip into. It was your mother asleep in that same bed you are in right now. I could see she was an Addison but not the one who captured me. For the first few nights, I watched her dreams. I needed to know what kind of person she was. If she was someone who would help me or if she was as crazy as her ancestor."

On one hand, that sounded like a really cool power. On the other, it sounded incredibly invasive. Angels probably weren't too worried about the latter. Plus, he had every right to be cautious. Her ancestor was a bitch. Who was to say they all weren't?

"Once I was sure your mother was a good person, I created dreams that allowed me to interact with her, and she thought it was all part of the dream. As I got to know her, I realized I actually liked her, so I took a leap and revealed everything to her. Thank goodness we were in a dream because when I told her who I was, she screamed and threw anything at me she could get her hands on. If it had been real life, she could have done some serious damage. Her aim was impressive. I had to let her exhaust herself enough to listen to me. She didn't believe me right away. I was patient, though. I visited her dreams day after day. Each time she would get more comfortable." He paused as he squished his face up.

"You might not want to hear this next part."

Great. He was going to talk about sex.

"By day your mother was searching her aunt's house for my book and by night she was in my arms in our dream world. I was happy. Almost enough to let things stay the way they were. Everything changed when your mom told me she was pregnant in real life."

Crazy angel dream daddy says what?

There's no way she heard him right. "I'm sorry. Are you saying you got her pregnant in the dream world and it manifested in the awake world, or whatever you want to call it?"

"Yeah, we were pretty surprised. Angels and humans having babies isn't unheard of. Creating it in the dream world... well, I'm not so sure about that."

"I always thought I had the most mundane life. Now you're telling me I may be the only one in existence? This just keeps getting better and better." She shook her head. At this point, she didn't know what to believe. "Let's say I choose to believe all this. What happened then?

"At first, nothing changed. She continued looking for a way to break me free. We had considered having her pray to another angel but decided we needed to keep you a secret until we knew if you were allowed to exist."

Well, that was a terrifying thought.

"Then the aunts started coming around. She said at first they were curious since she was a single woman not dating anyone. Then they accepted it and became extra attentive. Your mom didn't understand why until they did a spell and found out she was carrying a girl. She said they became agitated and pushed her to end the pregnancy. Going on and on about single women shouldn't be having babies and all that ridiculousness."

Adathan's mood shifted with the story. He was

angry as he continued. "Toward the end of our visits, I could see your mom was acting more and more erratic. There was nothing I could do. Then one day the visits stopped."

"So I was going to be the fourth Addison. They have to be the reason she ran away." She pictured her mother pregnant and scared on the run. No woman should have to do that to keep her baby. "She knew the aunts were too strong for her. Where did she go after she gave me up? Can you think of anything she might have said that would hint where she would hide?"

He sat silently, thinking, before shaking his head. "Not that I remember. We were mostly focused on freeing me. And to be fair, often there was no talking at all."

Ewe. Just ewe.

"It looks like I need to meet these aunts. Hang tight, my friends and I will get you out. And if anything happens to me, they know you are here and they won't give up."

She was a grown-ass adult. Would her aunts really do something to her now?

thirteen

OVER BREAKFAST, Addison filled the group in on everything she learned from Adathan. Nutmeg arrived in the middle of the discussion looking as bad as he had the day before.

He plopped down right in the middle of the table. "I still hear her and I still can't get through the barrier. What kind of husband am I to let myself forget her and then not be able to rescue her?"

Addison handed him a warm croissant. "Witches with angel powers did this to you. No one, especially Sasha, blames you for what happened. Yes, familiars are powerful, but you aren't untouch-able. I think you can take a pass on the guilt this once."

Xavier clapped his hands together. "So, what's our next move?"

Which of the situations did they take care of first? Addison took a deep breath to center herself. "I think we have to meet the aunts. We can make an unannounced visit. Catch them off guard."

Mr. Allan walked in. His face tense. "The Aunts... they're here. Coming up the drive now."

Minnie snorted. "Addison's must think alike."

Panic filled Addison. She wasn't ready. She thought she'd have a long drive to prepare herself.

Nutmeg jumped up, his hair standing on end.

Addison held out her hand to stop him. "We can't let on we know anything. We have to act clueless. Nutmeg, you can't reveal you have your memories back. If you don't think you can do that, I need you to hide until they're gone."

He gave her a hard stare and huffed. "Fine. I can control myself."

"Okay. Luna, can you tell Mrs. Allan to bring tea to the drawing room? Everyone else, paste on your friendliest smiles. I know that will be tough for you Minnie, and let's see if we can fool these witches."

They crossed the hall and tried to look nonchalant. Nutmeg curling up on Addison's lap felt like a bit much, but he knew these women better than she did.

Heels echoed through the entryway. Mr. Allan opened the door and let the aunts in. Addison now knew what she would look like when she was in her eighties. Thankfully, she holds up well. Both women looked like older versions of her, but their styles were slightly different. One was dressed in a blazer and matching long skirt. Her large hat made her head look ridiculously small. She was exactly what you would expect an eighty-year-old to look like. The other was in jeans and a flowery top. She had a lot of jewelry on and her makeup said she was ready for the club. Admittedly, it did make her look a lot younger than her sister.

There was a faint hint of surprise when they saw Nutmeg, but they hid it well behind bright smiles.

"So it's true. Our Addison has returned." The grandma one held her arms wide. Addison had no choice but to get up and hug her. Her light rose-scented perfume matched the rest of her.

"Okay, enough of that. It's my turn. Come here." The other aunt pulled her into an embrace. "What a relief to know you are alive and well."

Yeah... sure it was.

Addison pulled back and waved to the empty

couch across from everyone else. As they settled, Luna and Mrs. Allan came in with trays of tea and biscuits, or cookies, as they called them in America, which was totally freaking confusing.

The Aunts smiled brightly at the housekeeper. "It's been so long. You never gave up hope of their return."

Mrs. Allen was well aware of everything they'd learned so far from Adathan. She had a tight smile and simply nodded and left the room. It wasn't discreet, but it was better than outright accusing them.

Addison waited for Luna to sit and then started introductions. "These are my friends Luna, Minnie, Xavier, Skylar, and, of course, you know Nutmeg."

The elderly aunt clapped her hands together. "It's so good to see you, Nutmeg. I was so sad when our time came to an end. I'm surprised and happy that you were sent to a new Addison."

"Ads, it's been a while. You're looking good." He actually sounded friendly. "You too Addy."

So now they knew which witch was which. Say that ten times fast.

Addy nodded at him. "It's good to see you again."

There wasn't a hint of malice or subterfuge in

her voice. They deserved Oscars for their performances.

"So, Addison," Ads addressed the elephant in the room. "Tell us what you've been doing all this time. Why didn't you come home sooner and where's our sweet Addison?"

Addison took a deep breath. How in the world was Nutmeg staying so calm? "I didn't know about this place until two months ago. I didn't know anything about the magical world or that I was a witch. I was raised by a beautiful, caring woman who said my mother had come to her right after I was born and asked her to take me." There was no need to mention the acting crazy part, or that she wiped all their memories before disappearing. "I'm here hoping to find my birth mother. So far, we can't find any trace of her after she gave me up."

Ads clutched her chest. "Oh, you poor thing. I wish she had given you to us. You should have been raised by family."

Addy nodded. "We thought she was acting a little odd before she took off, but we never would have guessed she'd give you away. She must have been out of her mind. Sometimes pregnancy is too much."

Addison dug her nails into her palms to keep calm. "I can't speak to any of that. If you have any suggestions on where we could look for her, or spells we could try, we'd be grateful. She is alive. I feel it in my bones."

Addison didn't really feel anything. She wanted the aunts to feel that fear again of a potential fourth Addison being alive.

"We can go through our library and send over some things for you to try. I can sense the power in all four of you." Addy nodded toward Minnie and Luna, and then over to Skylar. "If you have done locator spells and came up empty, I wouldn't get my hopes up."

Ads glanced around the room. "I haven't been here in years. Have you had a chance to explore the grounds yet? Found anything interesting?"

So they wanted to know if she found the secret altar room that hid her dad. "We haven't had much time to explore. We've only been here a couple of days and jet lag really took a lot out of us. Do you know any good hidey spots we should explore?"

They shook their heads and shrugged. "It's a pretty standard magickal house. There are probably lots of good things in here. The fun is in the hunt, so we won't give away any secrets." Addy seemed genuine. If Addison hadn't talked to Adathan, she would never have suspected these two women of being evil.

Damn, they were good.

Addison had to be better.

fourteen

BEING A SECRET AGENT WAS EXHAUSTING. The aunts had stayed through the late afternoon. Addison never would have made it through if it weren't for Luna and Xavier. They were quite the charmers, and it was noteworthy that they were very touchy-feely with each other. That was going to make for a fun interrogation later.

Dinner should have been a time to celebrate them getting through the day, but everyone was too worn out. Taran had come and read the room enough to know they needed relaxation. He put on quiet music, helped Mrs. Allan make plates, and sat while everyone ate quietly.

Normally, after dinner, they would go to the library to research. Tonight, they needed a break.

Everyone went on their own and Nutmeg left to try again with Sasha.

She felt terrible they hadn't come up with an answer yet for him. Maybe tomorrow would be the day.

Addison dropped her head back against the dining room chair and stared up at the ceiling. "I never realized how simple my old life was. I can't believe your family willingly deals with all this drama."

Taran chuckled. "I know right now you feel like all of your ancestors are bad people. Even the first Addison, who we now know did a terrible thing. She saved my relative though, which means I'm standing here today. Your family has always helped the community in secret. There were years when crops were dying, or herds were getting sick. Your family stepped in and saved their neighbors without their knowledge and with no thanks. We have the lowest crime in the country, probably all of Europe. There never really seems to be repeat offenders and people who commit petty crimes like stealing food magickly get opportunities so they can better their situation."

She lifted her head and smiled at him. "Thank

you. I didn't know any of that and it does help to accept I'm a spawn of evil."

He stood up and held his hand out to her. "That was very dramatic. You need a change of scenery."

Her first instinct was to reject him. Something in his eyes said she belonged with him. Every time he was around, she did feel better. If she ever needed someone to take care of her, it was at this moment.

She took his hand and let him lead her toward the back of the house. He grabbed blankets from a closet and led her out the door and through the garden she still hadn't taken the time to tour.

The full moon gave enough light for them to walk easily through the field and finally stop at a lower cliff than they'd ridden to before. Taran let go of her hand to lay out a blanket over a large boulder. He sat down and leaned back against the rock. He shook out another blanket and put it over his legs. "It gets cold on the shoreline. Want to join me?"

She squinted at him. "This seems like a setup so you can get me to cuddle with you."

He shrugged. "Maybe, maybe not. Either way, you're going to love it if you do."

Tingles danced across her skin. There was that feeling again. The one she'd never experienced with her husband, or even when she thought she might like Xavier. This was an intensity her body starved for. She felt like she'd crawl out of her skin if she didn't get into his arms right then. It was frightening to take that step toward him. She wasn't an impulsive person, though. Why resist it?

She curled up next to him and even curled against his side. He wasn't kidding about the cold.

"Look up." He scooted down and laid his head back on the stone.

She copied his movement and gasped. Thousands of stars felt like they were close enough to touch. This is something she'd only seen in pictures. Light pollution ruined this for most people.

A shooting star streaked across the sky. Tears welled in her eyes. She felt truly relaxed for the first time in her life. All at once, she understood. This was where she was meant to be.

Why not give in to the impulses?

She sat up and kissed him. He froze in surprise and then gave in and kissed her back. And boy, was it a kiss. This was the type of kiss that curled your toes and tingled your scalp.

Of course, he smelled good. Why wouldn't he?

The man seemed damn near perfect. Almost like he was made just for her.

Maybe he was. No, her family wasn't that powerful, were they?

Taran pulled back. "I can practically hear you thinking. Stop contemplating and start enjoying. I'm trying to woo you, damn it."

"Well, I've never been wooed before. Carry on."

He cupped her cheek. "That's a damn shame. I promise to woo you every day for the rest of our lives."

Something melted. Maybe it was her heart, maybe it was her panties. Either way, she was putty in his hands.

The moon arched across the sky as they lay there kissing and talking. She now knew his favorite snack was pickles, which she tried to argue wasn't a snack. And he now knew hers was raw cookie dough, which he tried to argue wasn't a snack either.

By the time they walked home, the sun was almost up. She hadn't stayed up all night with a boy since she was seventeen.

He held the back door open for her and gave her a small bow. "I'm going to get a couple of hours of sleep, maybe a shower, and then I'll come see how Operation Rescue Everyone is going."

"Ha. That's a great name. I wish it weren't true, but yeah, we have three beings counting on us." Part of her didn't want to include her mom because that meant she had hope of her mother being alive. The other part of her was adamant she was, and she'd try manifesting the hell out of it if it would help. "I'll see you in a few hours."

They shared one last spine-tingling kiss before going their separate ways. She laughed as she thought again about his name for their operation. Then she gasped and ran for the secret altar room. Her poor angel maybe daddy was probably freaking out that she hadn't slept and visited him. That's what happened with her mother, after all.

Can angels have abandonment issues?

fifteen

IT HADN'T TAKEN Addison long to fall asleep. Staying up all night at forty-six will do that to a person. Adathan had been relieved to see her. Like she assumed, he had worried something had happened to her, too.

She told him about the aunt's visit and how sweet they were. He begged her not to underestimate them and then left her to sleep peacefully so she could get a couple of hours in before the craziness of whatever the new day would bring started.

Addison woke up to the alarm she'd set and went to find the rest of the crew. She found them in the drawing room, standing over something on the couch. When they backed away, she saw it was

Nutmeg. He had large patches of hair missing and he was moaning.

"I thought you two had bonded?" Minnie accused her.

"We are. We did the ceremony. What happened to him?

Minnie didn't give up. "You should have been able to feel him get this injured. Why didn't you know?"

"You think I know how any of this works?" She yelled back, defending herself. "I was in the altar room. Maybe it blocks the connection?" Her poor familiar had been out electrocuting himself while she made out under the stars.

Minnie seemed to accept her idea. "He stumbled in and passed out in the doorway. Luna did a spell to heal his worst injuries."

"These aren't the worst?" Now she really felt like shit. "You know what, forget this. Clarice!" She belled into the air. "Clarice, we need you right now."

A second later, the tiny fairy popped into the room. "Look, I can explain. They said I had to get rid of him. I didn't know what else to do. Please don't be mad. I didn't want to make him your problem again, I swear."

Addison glanced at the others, who all shrugged.

What on earth was she talking about? "Okay. So why did you do it?" This always worked with her sons. If they thought she already knew, they easily spilled the beans.

"They said he was driving everyone crazy, even the other prisoners. Since I didn't ask permission before putting him in there, they said I had to handle it. They transformed him into the flamingo and I made it a keychain for easy travel. Has he been giving you guys a hard time?"

Addison had to pick her jaw up off the floor, metaphorically speaking. "Oh my god. Are you talking about Malachi?" she turned to Luna. "Do you have it?"

Luna dug the keychain out of her pocket and held it up.

Clarice gasped. "You left him like that? That's just mean."

"We left him?" Addison snapped back. "Why on earth do you think we would have known?"

She twisted her hands in front of her. "You're all-powerful. I thought you'd be smart enough to sense it wasn't just a keychain."

Minnie stepped toward the fairy, who flew out of reach.

Clarice waved her hand, and the keychain transformed into a live, three-foot-tall flamingo. "It's about time. The least you could have done was leave me out where I could see things. Instead, you stuffed me in your pocket for days."

It was so odd hearing Malachi's voice come out of the bird. Luna was shaking her head back and forth. "Oh no. This isn't good. Now I know why I was drawn to the keychain. You're my familiar."

The flamingo's head cocked to the left. He walked in a circle around her. "It would seem you are correct. Clarice, what is the meaning of this?"

The fairy's cheeks were bright red. "That makes sense. I was wondering why they'd chosen an animal. I didn't know their plan. They must have known I would bring him to you all. You still have to serve your sentence. They've still limited your access to magic, but you know enough to still be useful to Luna."

Addison pinched the bridge of her nose. How did Luna, the sweetest witch in the world, end up with a cantankerous old man bird as a familiar? Every time she thought things couldn't get stranger, they did. She really needed to work on her manifesting abilities.

Clarice flew closer to Addison. "If you didn't know about him, why did you scream for me?"

She pointed at Nutmeg, who hadn't moved. "First, you are going to heal him. Second, you said you can portal anywhere. Portal us into the Rejected Familiars realm and help us save his wife." She pointed her head toward the flamingo. "You owe us."

Clarice's eyes widened. "I'm happy to heal him. You don't know what you're asking, though. That isn't a realm you pop in and out of. We'd be popping in completely blind." She flew back and forth, wringing her hands. "I'm already in so much trouble. This is expressly forbidden."

She seemed to contemplate quite a bit before sighing and flying over to Nutmeg. She laid her hand on his forehead and seconds later, his eyes fluttered open. The hair patches were already peach fuzz.

Addison scooped him up and hugged him. They weren't normally touchy-feely, but he looked close to death and she had let him face that on his own. "I'm so sorry. We're going to get Sasha, I promise."

"I'll do it, but if I get kicked out of the fae realm, I'm coming to live with you." Clarice's threat actually gave Addison a millisecond of pause. "Why not? I already have ghosts, what's a fairy."

"You have a sacred area outside, right? This is going to be a group effort. We need all the juice we can get." She opened a portal and flew through. Everyone followed suit, and they stepped outside of the altar area in the woods.

Addison glanced back at the house. "We could have walked. It's not that far."

Clarice shrugged. "This was more efficient. Now, I bear no responsibility for anything that may go wrong." She waited for each of them to nod at her. "Addison, keep hold of Nutmeg. Everyone else put a hand on him and channel your energy toward him. We're all going to think about Sasha so I can try to get as close to her essence as possible."

Skylar held a hand up. "Um, I've no idea what Sasha looks like."

"None of us do," Xavier said.

"Oh, she's beautiful. She looks a lot like me. She has thick brown fur and the most beautiful brown eyes." It was probably the first time Addison had ever heard Nutmeg talk lovingly about anything.

"Super helpful," Minnie mumbled as she put her hand on Nutmeg.

"I think you should hold me, too." Everyone looked down at the flamingo, staring up at Luna.

That's right, they have a flamingo now too why not?

Luna pursed her lips. Malachi pushed again.

"I'm your familiar. That means I can boost your power."

"Okay, okay." She held her arms out and scooped him up.

No one meant to burst into laughter. She looked too absurd not to.

"Okay, get it all out. Can we focus on the mission now?" Poor Luna had been hoping for a familiar. This couldn't have been what she wanted.

It took a minute to settle everyone down. When Malachi craned his neck to rest his head on her shoulder, the laughter started all over again.

Clarice was the first to settle down. "Okay, we're going to do this. Everyone focus on Sasha."

Addison tried to picture Nutmeg but with a bow in her hair and curly eyelashes. How else did you differentiate them?

A tingle started at the base of Addison's spine and traveled upward and into her hands. She pictured her power flowing into him.

The ground shook as the wind picked up.

"Hang on, I'm almost there," Clarice shouted.

A crack of lightning struck just outside the circle as a swirl of color appeared in front of them. "Okay, here goes."

Clarice flew at the portal and bounced off it like

a bug hitting a windshield. Nutmeg jumped from Addison's arms and ran for it. This was going to hurt.

He went straight through and disappeared. She walked up to the portal and reached out. Her hand hit an invisible barrier. "Luna, bring Malachi over here."

"I don't want to go in there," he argued.

"Relax, I just want to see if you can. Just stick a leg through or something."

Everyone held their breath as the scrawny bird's leg hesitantly stretched toward the portal and went straight into it. "Okay, okay. Pull me back." He sounded genuinely terrified. How bad was this place?

"Okay, so you got a door open, but only familiars can get through. That's okay. Nutmeg is tough. He's got this." Addison had to believe he would be fine because she didn't know what she'd do if not.

Twenty minutes later, she was ready to pull her hair out. Every few minutes, one of them had tested the barrier with no luck. How long could Clarice hold the door open?

"I vote we send bird brain in to find them," Minnie suggested.

Luna and Malachi gasped at the same time.

The door crackled, the colors becoming erratic. Was it going to close?

They fell backward as an animal came leaping through the doorway. Nutmeg on its shoulders with a triumphant smile on his face.

Clarice shut the door behind them.

"Really Nutmeg? You said she looked like you." Xavier was exasperated.

"She does? What are you talking about?" He absently pet his wife's head. "I hope you aren't implying something about her size?"

"She's a freaking bear. A bear and a groundhog don't look alike." Xavier shouted back. They did have the same color fur and her eyes were black, so Nutmeg hadn't been completely wrong.

"Huh, that explains why I had such a hard time locating her. He was picturing her, but all of you were picturing a groundhog."

"Hi everyone. Thank you for helping my little pooh bear find me." Sasha had a soft, melodic voice. It definitely belied her size.

"Can we all call him Pooh Bear from now on?" Minnie looked all too pleased to learn the new nickname.

Nutmeg rolled his eyes.

"I have a question." Skylar was the quiet type,

but when he did speak, he always had a good point or valid question. "How did you guys get your memories back?"

Sasha grabbed Nutmeg and pulled him in her large arms. "For me, it wasn't until this little furball came running at me and planted a big, wet kiss on me. Everything flooded back all at once."

Every head cocked to the side. Like Addison, they were probably trying to picture the tiny groundhog kissing the large bear.

It just goes to show you can't question love.

Nutmeg looked up at Sasha as he answered. "For me, it wasn't until I went to our home in the familiar realm. My friends dragged me to our house and showed me pictures. I grabbed a blanket that smelled like her and all my memories returned."

"At least we know now angel magic isn't ironclad."

Xavier had a good point. Maybe they did have a shot at releasing him.

Luna had reached out and touched Sasha and then quickly apologized. "Sorry, I've never been this close to a bear. I was thinking though, why did the aunts send you guys away?"

"They'd been using the angel magick to block parts of themselves from us. We didn't know anything about the angel. We accidentally found the book he'd given the original Addison. We questioned them and they admitted everything to us. We demanded they tell your mom and that's when they decided to get rid of us."

"Well, I'm going to head home and see if I'm in trouble. Hopefully, I won't be back soon." Clarice waved and disappeared into a tiny portal.

"I think we could all use a little break and give Nutmeg and Sasha time to catch up." Addison wished she could warn Mrs. Allen about the incoming bear. Then again, if Sasha had been with Addy before, then it should be no surprise.

One hostage down, one to go. She wouldn't count her mom a hostage since they didn't even know if she was alive.

Addison stayed in the back of the group and watched everyone joking and laughing as they walked back to the house. For the first time in days, Addison actually felt good. Maybe they could pull this off.

sixteen

ADDISON STARED at the text message. "I can't believe it. Leo and Francesca already found a body and Ava can come tomorrow to do the ritual."

"That's great. I'm so happy for them." Luna tossed a shrimp at Malachi, who was curled up on the chair next to her.

"Why don't you sound excited?" Taran already knew her too well.

"They haven't been together that long. What if it doesn't work out?"

"Seriously?" Minnie looked exasperated. "If it doesn't work out, they go their separate ways and Francesca still gets a second chance at life."

That sounded good in theory, to Addison. Magick was never that easy, though. "Maybe, but I got the impression this would only work if she linked them together. I would imagine something bad would happen if they broke up."

"Oh, well, that is a risk." Minnie sipped her drink and looked anywhere but at Addison.

"Don't listen to her," Luna glared at the terrible emotional support witch. "Love is a gamble. Sure, they have more riding on the line than the average couple. That doesn't make it any different. They are going to have a lot of work ahead of them, and you'll be right there to help them."

"You're right. I'm just a nervous mom and I feel like I'm Francesca's mom, too. She needs someone to look out for her." It was nerves. That's all it was. Luna was right. They had to take a chance on love and work hard to make it last. And she would be right there to make sure her son never treated Francesca like his father treated her.

Mrs. Allan walked into the dining room hesitantly. "You wanted to talk to Mr. Allan and I after dinner. Is now a good time?"

She looked like she was walking to her death. The poor woman was petrified. Addison really spoke before understanding the dynamics of their world.

She gave her friendliest smile and waved them in. "Absolutely. Come on in."

Mr. Allan held a chair out for his wife and then sat next to her. They clutched hands like they were each other's lifeline. He spoke first. "I heard about your conversation with Mrs. Allan. We'll do anything you ask if you'll let us stay here. We can even stay in a cabin far from the main house. We love it here and we love your family and want to stay nearby."

"Man, I really mucked all of this. Please don't be upset. I'm not sending you away. We don't need to change anything if you don't want to. However, I don't think your situation is fair. Xavier and Skylar helped me look into it. I can release the bond that forces you to stay on property. I can pay you a decent wage and paid vacation days and sick time. You showed me the family ledger. You know we can afford it."

Mrs. Allan let out a yowling sob and fell into her husband's arms.

Was that a good cry or a bad one?

He rubbed her back gently as he spoke to Addison. "Your generosity is unlike anything seen in our world. If we told the other elves, there would probably be a revolt."

"Maybe there should be," Xavier interjected.

Mr. Allan shrugged. "I don't know about all

that. Our lot is happy with the lives we have. But if you insist on these changes, we won't stop you. We'll continue to work for you as long as you'll have us."

Addison wilted in relief. "Phew. I thought you were going to be a much harder sell. Thank you for making this easy. I'll work on getting everything set up as soon as I'm done dealing with my angel daddy, crazy aunts, and a missing mother."

They nodded their thanks and left. Mrs. Allan could still be heard when they were out of sight. "Wow. Elves take their jobs very seriously."

Everyone nodded in agreement.

"I personally think what you're doing is irresponsible." Malachi's pink head popped up. "There's a natural order to things and you shouldn't go messing with it."

"Malachi, do you like shrimp?" Luna asked sweetly.

"Of course I do. I liked them as a human, but as a flamingo, I crave them."

"Well, if you ever want another one, you'll keep thoughts like that to yourself."

Wow, go Luna.

The flamingo's head sank back under the table without a word.

Addison had been worried Luna couldn't handle Malachi. She seriously underestimated her friend.

Her cell phone rang loudly, making her jump. "Oh shoot. It's time for my Facetime with Mom and the boys. I'll see you guys in a bit."

She rushed out of the room and into the library. Her family's faces appeared on the screen as she answered. Tears welled in her eyes. This was the longest and farthest she'd ever been from them and she could really use a hug from her mom, too.

"Addison."

"Mom."

"Ma."

"Hey guys, it's so good to see you. How's everyone doing?"

Iggy spoke first. "Come on. We're fine. We want to talk about you. Leo mentioned a man?"

Theresa jumped in. "Minnie told Francesca he's gorgeous and you're engaged?"

She shouldn't have been surprised they knew. It was really good gossip. If it wasn't about her, she'd want to talk about it too. "His name is Taran. He says our mothers promised us to each other. Obviously, that doesn't mean anything, so it's not a big deal."

Fitz snorted. "Luna told Francesca that you guys

make lovey eyes at each other and disappeared the other night for a while."

Okay, that happened after Francesca was there. "What the hell? Francesca is still a ghost, right? How is she in constant communication with my friends?"

"They have a group chat on Leo's phone and he does all the texting for her," Iggy answered with a cheesy smile.

"Okay. I feel like everyone is way too invested in my love life."

There was a quiet knock at the door. Taran popped his head inside. "Minnie said you wanted to see me."

Addison glared at the phone screen. "I guess they aren't the only ones with a group chat, are they?"

Theresa ignored the question. "Well, he's there now. Let us meet him."

She turned back to Taran. "If you'd like to meet the rest of my family, you are welcome. You absolutely don't have to if you don't want to."

He strolled in and grabbed the phone right out of her hands. "Hey everyone. It's nice to meet you."

"Oh my god, that accent." Theresa tried to whisper, but she was really bad at it.

Taran laughed it off. "I'm sure this has been

weird for all of you. I promise I'm not going to kidnap her and make her marry me."

Addison wasn't sure how her boys were going to react.

Laughter and jokes were not at the top of the list. In a matter of minutes, Taran had charmed them.

Damn, he was good.

And that was perfectly fine with Addison.

seventeen

ADDISON WAITED by the gate for Leo and his guests to arrive. Right on time, the portal opened and Drew walked out, followed by Ava, Olivia, Leo, and Francesca. She expected the portal to close and was shocked to see Iggy, Fitz, and Theresa walk out, too. Why was she not surprised?

What did surprise her was a long box come hovering through. The realization that a young woman had to be dead for this to happen really sunk in.

Ava smiled solemnly. "I can assure you we took every care to be respectful. You have a good son. He had a small ceremony for her and Olivia donated money to a lupus foundation in her name."

Tears stung Addison's eyes. This was really happening. "And she had no family?"

Leo grabbed her hands. "We watched her for a couple of days and asked the hospital staff. No one had ever come to visit her. She'd been on the transplant list for a long time. Now she will get to live on in Francesca."

He really was a good man. "Okay. We'll have to do the drive in shifts."

A noise in the field had everyone turning. Mr. Allan was rolling up in an ancient-looking truck. "I thought you could use the help."

She mouthed thank you to him as the casket was floated over and gently set in the truck's bed. The three boys jumped in. "We'll ride with her. The rest of you go with Mom."

The short ride up to the house was a solemn one. Her friend's faces when they pulled up matched hers when she first saw it. What did they all think was going to happen? They should have prepared themselves a little better for this.

Ava gently touched Addison's shoulder. "It might be most comfortable for Francesca if she were lying in a bed when the joining happens."

"Of course. Follow me." Her feet were heavy as she led the group up the stairs and to the first empty bedroom. "Unless you need help, I think it would be best if we wait out here while you get everything situated."

"We got this." Drew gave her an understanding smile as he went into the room. She was surprised to see Iggy and Fitz offer their help. Leo said no and then hugged them. She hadn't seen her boys hug since they were kids. It added to the heaviness of the moment.

"Leo, where's Francesca?" Addison hadn't seen her since they arrived.

A second later, she appeared next to him. Her eyes were red-rimmed. "I'm sorry for hiding. I want this more than anything. I'm having a hard time processing this next part."

"You are honoring Monica by living for her. It was her time to go. Her spirit moved on. She had no unfinished business. You have nothing to feel guilty about." Ava's words helped Addison as much as they did Francesca. How hard it must be being a necromancer and dealing with death all the time.

A minute later, the door opened again and Drew nodded at them to come in. The girl was dressed in a beautiful lace dress. She was painfully thin. Even in that state, she was beautiful. Addison could see a slight resemblance to Francesca.

Ava handed Leo a necklace with a thin shard of stone hanging from it. "You'll have to wear this at all times. It is like a small battery that will keep the connection between you strong. Francesca, are you ready?"

She solemnly nodded and lay on the bed next to Monica. The room was silent as Ava moved her hands, working with magick they couldn't see. One second Francesca was there and the next she wasn't.

Addison panicked and leaped forward. Minnie and Luna pulled her back. A few more words and gestures from Ava and Monica gasped awake. The girl looked down at her new body. In the process of joining them, the body had been healed. She looked like a healthy twenty-year-old again.

Francesca grabbed her boobs. "Oh, I missed having these. Thank you, Monica." She leaped from the bed and almost fell. Leo was there to catch her. For the first time, they were touching.

Olivia cleared her throat. "How about we give these two a few minutes? We'll wait downstairs to make sure all is well."

Addison wiped the tears from her cheeks. "Yes, of course. I think we could all use a strong drink."

The group quietly filed back downstairs and followed Addison to the library, where the good liquor cabinet was. She hadn't prepared them for the paintings of all of her reincarnations.

"What in the world?" Olivia walked slowly around, studying them as closely as Addison had.

"I didn't mean to bring this up, but now I realize you all might be able to help us. What do you know about angels?"

She gave them credit. Their surprise was barely noticeable.

"How about we get that drink and you can give us more details." Drew took a glass from Xavier and sat down.

When everyone was settled, Addison began. "You asked us to keep the secret of what you can do. In return, I ask that you keep what I'm about to tell you a secret as well. A very long time ago, my ancestor trapped an angel in that room back there and has been siphoning his powers ever since. Before he was sealed away, he cursed her to reincarnate every generation and when four Addison's were alive at the same time, the fourth would have the power to free him." She really loved the look of shock on their faces. It truly was an incredible story. "Fast forward to forty-six years ago. My mom didn't know about the prisoner behind the wall. She fell asleep in the room and he was able to talk to her in her dreams. They fell in love and made me and somehow the pregnancy manifested in the real world too. I've been talking to my dad in my dreams and he said I had the power to release him with blood magic. The problem is, we can't find any books referencing anything even close to what we're dealing with."

She paused and took a sip of the wine Luna had handed her.

"Wow, and I thought our family was crazy." Ava chuckled.

"Luci could probably just pop in and free him, right?" Drew asked.

"Who's Luci?"

Ava smiled mischievously. "Oh Lucifer, the King of Hell, he's Olivia's dad. So don't think you are alone in having major daddy issues."

Crazy necromancer says what?

Minnie tugged on Skylar's arm. "She did say Lucifer as in Satan, right?"

Olivia rolled her eyes at her friends. "It's not that big of a deal. You know I don't want to bother him while he and mom are on vacation. Did you try cutting yourself and bleeding on the spot where he was sealed?"

Addison cocked her head. Everyone looked back and forth at each other.

"Could it really be that easy?" Addison was going to be so mad if that's all she had to do. She was kind of hoping for some cosmic battle.

Olivia shrugged. "No idea. It seems to me you should try the obvious first. If that doesn't work, let us know and we'll do some research on our side. We'll exhaust every other possibility before we get Luci involved."

Who were these people? They were incredible.

Ava gulped down the last of her drink and stood up. "We haven't heard anything from the new couple, so I'm going to assume we're all good. If anything changes, Olivia can have us here in minutes."

Taran set his glass down. "I'll drive them to the gate and take myself home." He bent and kissed the top of Addison's head. "See you tomorrow."

When it was only her friends and family left in the room, it erupted. They acted like middle schoolers seeing someone kiss for the first time. "Oh my god guys, grow up." Her cheeks burned with embarrassment. At her age, she shouldn't still blush over a simple kiss. Where was a panicked person needing help when you needed a distraction?

eighteen

BREAKFAST the next morning was a glimpse into what Addison's life could be. Around the large table were her friends, Taran, her boys, the newly alive Francesca, a groundhog, a bear, and a flamingo. It was loud and chaotic, and it made her heart sing.

When the last dish was cleared, the room got silent. Minnie tossed her napkin on the table. "So, what's the plan? Go bleed on a wall for Daddy or drive to the aunts and poke around?"

Addison weighed the options. "It makes sense to try freeing Adathan first. If he gets out, he can help with the aunts."

Minnie held out her knife, covered in jam. "No time like the present."

Luna's face scrunched up. "Ewe. I'm sure we can get a clean one from the kitchen."

"The altar room has a few fancy-looking knives. Maybe they are really old and have a bit of magic in them. I'll take all the help I can get."

The chairs scraped across the floor as the group got up and made their way to the library. They gathered in a large semi-circle around the door, cheering her on. All curse breakers should have their own cheer squad.

She took a few steps inside and turned to wave at the group. Why was this so weird? Right, because she was trying to release an angel.

Butterflies danced in her belly as she approached the wall with Adathan's outline on it. Several knives were strewn around the room. She did as she was taught and opened her senses. The magic in the room was overwhelming, almost suffocating. Each of the knives was glowing with different intensities. She grabbed the brightest one, which was also the plainest one. It was the length of her hand, pewter, with a purple stone at the hilt. Even though it looked old, the edges of the blade gleamed in the candlelight.

She pushed the table out of the way and stared up at the wall. Was he really behind the stones? If she had been in the original Addison's shoes, would she have done the same thing? She hoped not. If being all-powerful meant imprisoning another person, then she didn't want that magick.

"Okay, here goes nothing." She held her hand up and sliced a diagonal line across her palm. "Owe, shit, that hurts." It made more sense to cut the top of her hand or her arm. It had to hurt less. That wasn't how they did it in the movies though, so who was she to challenge it? She needed all the luck she could get.

She squeezed her hand a few times to get a puddle. How much blood was enough? She had no idea. They'd never found an instruction manual.

"Ancestors, hear my prayer. Help me make right the wrong we have committed." The air around her felt heavy. She turned and saw the outlines of many past Addison's. They all put a hand on another's shoulder and the ghost closest to her put her icy hand on Addison. Tears stung her eyes. Not all the Addison's had been bad.

She reached toward the wall and slapped her hand right in the center of the sigil. Her blood snaked out from her hand to fill every crevice the mark was on. The lines glowed for a second before there was a blinding white light and an explosion that sent her flying backward. As she passed out, she prayed the ritual had worked.

Everything was fuzzy, and Addison's head was pounding. She could hear people screaming her name and a softer voice nearby. It was painful to open her eyes like she had stared at the sun for too long.

Slowly, the outline of a man came into focus. A beautiful man with blonde curls and golden eyes stared down at her. "Addison, you did it. You freed me." He touched her forehead and all the pain went away. "Sorry about that. When the bonds broke, my angel form burst free. Humans can't look at our true form or it will blind them. As soon as I realized what was happening, I went back into this form."

She took his hand and let him pull her up. "Adathan? You're real? I mean, I know we've been talking, but part of me was skeptical of the whole thing."

Her name was still being yelled from far away.

"Maybe we should tell your family you're okay."

"I'm fine. I'm coming out." She yelled back. Looking around the room, she was shocked at the destruction. The Addison ghosts were all gone and rubble from the wall had flown around the room, smashing anything in its way. This was a mess for another time.

Adathan stayed a step behind her as she walked back into the library. She was pulled into hugs, everyone talking at once. When Adathan stepped out, everyone froze.

What did you say to an angel?

Theresa curtsied. The boys followed suit and bowed. As Fitz went down, he said "Your Highness". Iggy wasn't much better with "My lord."

Adathan held his hands up to stop them. "Please call me Adathan. Don't treat me any differently than you would if I were human."

"Addison," Taran still looked concerned. "Are you okay? There was a bright light and an explosion that rocked the whole house."

"Ah, that's my fault." Adathan chimed in. "I wasn't in control when the binds broke and my angel form burst forward. I apologize for scaring anyone."

Taran stared at Addison, waiting for her to answer. Sweet of him to not cower to Adathan.

She brushed off her dusty clothes. "I'm no worse for wear. I had been knocked around, but he healed me immediately. Do you think you can all behave while I take ten minutes to shower and change clothes?"

Did she really trust them with Adathan? Could he handle that group? Minnie was surprisingly quiet in the back of the group. It was weird to not hear her snarky comments. Addison paused next to her. "You good?"

Her eyes widened. "That's a freaking angel. They're real? Like this is insane. I knew you were going to be a handful when I was assigned to you. This is next level though."

She patted her friend's shoulder. "I'm glad my life is entertaining for you. I'll be back in a minute."

Addison paused at the door and looked back. They were treating Adathan like he was a celebrity. He looked up and nodded at her. He would be fine.

She let out a ragged breath as she realized there was only one thing left to do. It was time to find out what happened to her mother.

nineteen

TEAM RESCUE EVERYONE sat around the dining room table. By the time Addison had come back from her shower, everyone had relaxed and had filled Adathan in on anything Addison had forgotten to tell him. Her boys had been showing him their cellphones and the games they could play on it.

Now it was time to talk business. "Adathan, I'm sure you've had a while to think about this. What do you want to do first?"

The smile fell from his face. "I have a question for you. If your aunts were to perish today, would that upset you?"

Her eyes darted around to see the myriad of

emotions on everyone else's faces. "Perish, so die? Well, I have no attachment to them, so in general, I wouldn't be too upset. However, they are still people, so I don't really condone murdering them."

He nodded as he thought for a second. "What if they make me? What if I confront them and we fight and they perish in battle?"

Were they really sitting here talking about murder? "Wow, really getting into semantics here. They knew about you. They tried to have me aborted, and they tortured my mom through her pregnancy. They deserve to be punished. If we confront them and they put up a fight, then what happens, happens."

She looked around the room again. Everyone seemed in agreement.

"Now that we've settled that. What would you like to do?"

The room spun as they were pulled through a vortex and landed in a drawing room she didn't recognize.

"What on Earth?" Her aunts ran into the room and stopped short when they saw the entourage of people standing there. "Addison? What is the meaning of this?"

How did she answer that? This hadn't been her idea. Everyone turned and parted ways to let Adathan walk forward.

The aunts gasped.

"Is that?"

"No, it's not possible."

"So you know who I am?" Adathan sounded surprisingly calm.

"What? No, who are you?" Addy wasn't fooling anyone.

Thunder rumbled outside. Adathan's hands were fisted at his side. He was losing his calm.

Addison stepped forward. "We came to tell you it's over. Adathan is taking his power back. It never belonged to us. You should have freed him as soon as you found out about him. That's what my mother tried to do, and it's what I did do."

For the first time, their demeanors changed. The friendliness was gone. Ads sneered at her. "How dare you. You shouldn't even exist. The spell should never have allowed you to be created."

This was news to Addison. "What spell?"

"After his prophecy, one of the past Addisons placed a spell over the family to prevent a fourth Addison from being created. The magic should have made you a boy." Addy accused her like it was her fault.

"I guess the spell didn't consider the father being an angel." Addison was proud to see the shock on their faces. So, they didn't know everything.

"You mean…" Ads looked between Adathan and Addison.

"That's not possible." Addy insisted.

Adathan smiled broadly. "I admit it wasn't planned. When I visited her mother in her dreams, I never thought we'd fall in love or make a child. Fate must be stronger than magick."

Addy roared and threw her arms out. Electricity shot from her fingers and hit Adathan square in the chest. Ads sent a giant hand across the room. It grabbed him and pinned him to the wall. Shadows rose from the corners of the room and raced at the aunts.

"Taran, protect my family," Addison yelled over the noise of the spells being flung around.

He nodded and grabbed her mother, three sons, and Francesca and pulled them to a corner of the room. Xavier joined him, standing shoulder to shoulder, blocking her family from harm. They would both get a big hug and kiss when this was over. Assuming they all made it out alive.

The windows burst open as vines snaked inside and wrapped around Adathan's throat. He hadn't severed the link between them, so they still had his extra power. It was two against one. Addison wasn't going to stand for that.

She focused on the bookshelves, attempting to send the large tombs at the women. Her magick still wasn't perfect, so instead of books flying, the pages ripped free and flew at them like razor blades. They screamed as hundreds of tiny paper cuts criss-crossed their bodies.

Water came rushing through the open windows and knocked down Addison and the others. Until then, the others had stayed out of the fight. They were letting Adathan get all his anger out. Soaking Minnie crossed a line.

She screeched as she got to her feet. She whispered a spell as crows flew into the windows and pecked at the women. Luna and Skylar were trying to free Adathan. They managed to get his mouth free. "Addison, you need to break the tether. Only an Addison can do it."

He couldn't have warned her about that sooner. "I don't know how."

"Use your senses, see the tether, and then cut

the shit out of it," Minnie yelled as she fought back a vine that snaked at her.

Sure, calm myself in this madness and focus on my senses. After a few deep breaths, she saw the faint golden light streaming from Adathan and branching off to Addison and the two aunts.

"Okay, cut it." She looked around the room and saw a sword above the fireplace. "Taran, can you reach that?"

Her hunky Scotsman easily pulled it from the wall and rushed it over to her. "You got this."

She nearly fell over as the weight of the sword surprised her. She dragged it to the place where the three branches converged and lifted the sword. The first swing was weak and bounced right off the tether. The second wasn't much better. The sword was too heavy.

Taran's arms came around hers. His hands grabbed the hilt below hers. Together, they lifted the sword high over her head and swung it with all their might. She thought about Adathan in prison and her mom terrified and pregnant as the blade sliced cleanly through the tether. Addison gasped as she felt the magic get pulled from her body. The spells the aunts were doing immediately stopped, their screams making everyone cover their ears.

Light filled the room as the magick returned to Adathan. He was full power now and even Addison was a little afraid of what he'd do next.

The aunts were lifted into the air. An invisible binding wrapped around them, pinning their arms down. "Do you know what's saddest about all of this? The first Addison had strengthened her own magick. Each time she reincarnated, she got stronger. You could have released me at any time, lost the connection to my magic, and still been powerful on your own."

"We didn't know or we would have released you ourselves." Ads pleaded with him.

"I highly doubt that. Now, tell me why my Addison ran away? And remember, I haven't decided your punishment. The longer it takes to get the truth out of you, the longer and more painful it will be."

That would have made Addison tell him anything he wanted to know. She had to hope the aunts were smart.

Ads was the first to break. The fight went out of her as she went limp. "When she wouldn't abort the baby, we tried to make her miscarry. We gave her potions and spelled her. Nothing seemed to work.

She grew more paranoid as the days went by. We didn't expect her to flee."

"Did you go after her?" He asked between clenched teeth.

Addy was quiet until the binds tightened around her and she screamed again before finally giving in. "Yes. It took months. By the time we'd found her, she'd already had the baby and gotten rid of it. We tried everything to get her to tell us where the baby was, but she had taken a potion that wiped her memory."

Addison rushed forward. "Wait, you saw her after she gave me up?"

Adathan cocked his head to the side as if listening to something. The air around the room spun like it had before, and they were transported to a dark hallway with no windows.

Adathan walked confidently forward and stopped in front of a metal door. He grabbed the handle and ripped it right off the hinges. He created a small ball of light and sent it into the room.

Addison rushed forward to look over his shoulder. In the corner, a woman was huddled over a desk sketching. The walls were covered in drawings of Adathan and a baby Addison had to assume was her.

She tried to rush forward. Adathan stopped her. "We need to take this slow."

He walked quietly forward and called her name gently. She didn't react until he put his hand over hers. She screamed and jumped out of the chair, running to the other side of the room and curling into a ball on a tiny bed.

"Addison, it's me. You're safe now." He kneeled down in front of the bed. "Look at me, love."

She slowly peaked between her fingers. You knew the second she recognized him because she flew into his arms. "You. You're the man I dream about."

The ball of light flew closer, and they got their first look at her. You could tell it was an Addison but just barely. Her hair was thin and stringy. It was horrifying to see she was skin and bone.

Addison walked up and kneeled next to Adathan. Her mom looked at her, studied her face. She glanced at the pictures on the wall and then again at her. "You're the baby?"

Tears poured down Addison's face. "Yes, I'm your daughter."

"She didn't start this way." Addy was still bound by the doorway. At hearing her voice, Addison's mom screamed and curled into a ball again.

Adathan waved his hand, and the aunts disappeared.

"Forget everything I said earlier. You do what you feel is best to them." Addison didn't care if that made her a bad person. "Is there anything you can do for her?"

Adathan reached out and touched her forehead. A bright light filled the room. When it faded away, her mother was still dirty, but also beautiful. Her hair fell in long curls down her back. Her skin was smooth and her body had filled out.

"Adathan? You're here?" She sat up and leaped into his arms.

He looked over at Addison as he held her mother. "I was able to undo the potion. Her memories are back."

"Mom?" Addison's voice trembled.

Her mother's beautiful eyes found hers. "My baby girl. I knew that woman would protect you. I don't know how you found your way back here."

Addison pointed at Adathan. "He said it was fate."

"This is beautiful and all, but it smells rank down here. Can you take us somewhere else?" Leave it to Minnie to bring everyone back to reality.

The room spun as the group disappeared and

reappeared in the dining room where they had started.

Her mother gasped and covered her mouth. "My house. It's just like I left it."

"I'll have dinner-" Mrs. Allan froze when she saw the older Addison. The pot of tea she was holding fell to the floor. It was stopped right before smashing. A room full of a wizard, witches, and an angel weren't going to let that happen. Mrs. Allan ran over, sobbing as she went. She crushed the older Addison into her arms and then turned and pulled Addison into a hug. "Thank you for bringing her home."

Her mother was probably exhausted, but there were people she needed to meet first. She grabbed Theresa and pulled her over. "Mom, I want you to meet my other mother, Theresa."

Older Addison pulled Theresa in for a hug. "I knew from your pain that day that you would go to the ends of the earth to protect my baby. I can see you've done a wonderful job."

Theresa choked on a sob. "It's nothing, really. She was a gift. You saved me that day as well."

Addison waved at the boys to walk over. "And these handsome guys are your grandsons. This is Fitz, Iggy, and Leo."

Her mother pulled each of them into a hug. "It is so wonderful to meet you."

Over their shoulder, she noticed Taran. "I would recognize you anywhere. You're Maggie's son, aren't you? Are you my son-in-law yet?"

It had only been thirty minutes and her mom was already embarrassing her. The best part is, she wouldn't want it any other way.

ADDISON LAUGHED as she passed around the picture of Mr. and Mrs. Allan as they posed in front of Niagara Falls. It was all a part of their world vacation. They were owed decades of vacation days.

Her mother and father, which still sounded weird to say, were gone on a honeymoon of sorts. The time to figure out what they were officially and who would live where would all be figured out later.

Addison, her sons, Theresa, Francesca, and Alexander packed up their lives and moved to the family house in Scotland. Everything that had happened with Addison and her mom had really affected the boys. They had considered staying in America, but didn't want to be that far from her.

Plus, it was a mansion in Scotland. Who wouldn't want to live there?

Her friends had all gone home, but Luna and Xavier were already back, and this time they were there as a couple. Even Malachi the flamingo had come and he was much better behaved than he was as a human.

Taran handed her a glass of wine. "Everything worked out in the end, didn't it?"

As for the betrothal, it was still on. It was just going to be a long engagement as they got to know each other.

Addison leaned over and gave him a small kiss. "I didn't think we were going to pull it off. And I couldn't have done it without all of you."

Luna held her glass up in agreement. "I do have a question, though. If there's an Addison every generation, where is your daughter?"

Eyes darted back and forth as everyone contemplated the question.

Addison scoffed. "I'm in perimenopause. I can't get pregnant."

"Did a doctor confirm that or was that your guess as to why your magick revealed itself?" Luna shot back.

Well, damn. Addison opened and closed her

mouth as she tried to think of the answer. "Adathan would have ended the reincarnation curse, right?"

There's no way her dad would do that to her, would he?

"Oh, FU-"

***

If you enjoyed the Chronicles of Addison Schmidt you should check out my other stories. I'm a sucker for an odd shifter!

Visit www.cassidykoconnor.com to purchase directly from me

If you want to learn more about Ava, Drew, and Olivia, you should check out the Witching After Forty series by Lia Davis and L.A. Boruff

Cassidy and her family recently relocated to the North Georgia Mountains after a lifetime in the Tampa Bay, Florida area. She's on a new adventure and loving every minute of it.

She loves reading and going to the movies, but not nearly as much as she enjoys traveling and hopes to one day watch a baseball game in every MLB stadium in the country.

She also writes under the pen name C.K. O'Connor. Books by C.K. range from sweet romance to young adult to historical romance.

To learn more about C.K. / Cassidy please visit her online at

www.cassidykoconnor.com.

You can also find her on Facebook at

https://www.facebook.com/CK-OConnor-Author-101376192171379

OR

www.facebook.com/cassidykoconnorauthor

Accepting Love

Resisting Love

Mending Love

<u>Forgiving Love</u>

<u>Fearing Love</u>

<u>Stand Alones</u>

Gruff Love

Sexy In White

To Steal a Prince's Heart

Wicked Wonderland Retreat Box Set

9 781949 575934